TYSON

A SAINT OR SINNER NOVEL

KATHY COOPMANS

Model: Ryan Vandyke

Photographer: Eric David Battershell

Cover Design by: Sommer Stein

Proofread by: Jill Sava

Editor: Julia Goda Editing Services

Formatting: CP Smith

To Ryan- Giving up is not an option.

TYSON

PROLOGUE

LYNNE

Whispering waves crash against the shore. It's hushed; gentle sounds are comforting as if they're singing a soulful lullaby.

The sky is ablaze with color. Fiery oranges, blazing reds paint the horizon as I imagine the yellow sun dipping into the ocean.

The sunset is more beautiful than my thoughts are capable of embracing these days as I lie in bed preparing for the biggest fight of my young life. *Alone.*

I feel my insides sinking with the sun. My heart drowning and my life dissipating with every tight breath I wish I didn't have to take. It hurts to breathe.

I never knew what heartbreak was. Deceit, lies, and cheating, yes. I'm used to living with those. My parents are the king and queen of dishonesty. However, to have my heart being ripped out of my chest with little or no chance of replacing it again is something I can't live with.

God help me. I really want to die.

Maybe I should be thankful it's happening now instead of years down the road. At least that's what my parents said.

Their words have torn me beyond recovery. Cut deeper than the scar that will soon be a reminder of why I'm here. Why I hurt and why I've lost him.

I was supposed to be getting married yesterday. Disappear from the cruel world I was raised in, to live a dream with the man I love instead of the life of the rich and famous.

Treachery. Lies. So many lies that unless you've lived it, you wouldn't believe it existed.

And here I am, not married, not happy, and unwilling to talk about it. No one would listen to me anyway. The youngest daughter of a world-known lawyer and his high standard noble Hollywood wife.

Doesn't matter now; nothing does. It's done. I listened to them, and they were right. The man I will forever love won't have the burden or feel the guilt or resent me later on. Typical fallen angel life.

I have to focus on what's happening to me now; the pain in my chest, the burn behind my eyes, and the sting of the needle as the nurse slips it into my arm is breaking my heart in a whole other way. It's my world changing for the rest of my life. It's the end of dreams. The end of hope and the end of happiness.

God help me. I really want to die.

Unconsciousness is coming slowly, pulling me under in small bits and pieces. I'm struggling to stay awake for fear I will forget him. The way his lips felt against mine. His chiseled jaw, broad shoulders, and soul-stealing smile.

Breathe, Lynne. One, two, three breaths, four.

I flinch; my eyelids are growing heavy. A lone tear escapes knowing that when I close my eyes, he'll be gone.

I feel numb. I feel pain.

I love you, Tyson.

I allow myself to drift, not to care whether I live or die.

CHAPTER ONE

TYSON

Thirteen years later

"Let me make this very clear, you rotten punk. You're dealing on my Goddamn streets. I do not give a fuck why you're doing it. The point is you are. Now, I'm asking you one more time to tell me who you're buying this shit from." My face is less than two inches away from this well-groomed, limp dick motherfucker, and he doesn't even flinch. I'd love to be able to bash his head up against this cement wall, drive my fist into his mouth, and kick his ass until he requires medical attention to sew his lips back onto his face. The cocky bastard. I hate lousy people who think they can bend the law to their advantage, then break it and continue to walk the streets as if life owes them a fucking favor when life doesn't owe anyone jackshit. You earn what life gives you, and this asshole is about to be paid with a life behind bars.

I've been home from a much-needed hiatus from my screwed-up life for two weeks now. Those entire two fucking weeks I've been searching from here to Bumfuck, Idaho, for this piece of shit who in his high-as-a-kite mind sold cocaine to an eighteen-year-old college student a few months back. Whatever he laced it with caused the drugged-up young woman to become so high she actually thought she could fly. Imagine that. Fuck!

Thank God, a couple of her friends had found her before she decided to attempt her flying skills off an overpass that would not only have killed her by splattering body parts all over. It would have caused a major wreck on the highway. Possibly killing or injuring several more people in the process, and this money-hungry punk has the gall to sit here with a smile on his face over it. Well, he has no idea what's about to rain down on his hundred-dollar light blue yuppie as fuck polo shirt with the collar turned up. I suppose he has matching deck shoes, too. I take a chance, look down, and sure as shit, he does. Damn. He isn't going to last an hour on the block before someone claims his ass.

"I'm not telling you shit, pig. I want my lawyer." Hell, no. He did not just decide to lawyer up. Shit don't go down that way with me. Not today and definitely not with the likes of him.

"It's cool. You can call him. You better pray like a whore being fucked in the face by her worst nightmare that he comes before any of us are through with you. 'Cause the way I see it"—I place my hands on both sides of the chair he's sitting in, lean my head up to his ear, and whisper—"I have less than five minutes before an FBI agent walks through that door, and that's plenty of time for me to break a few fingers. Might shove your balls up your ass, too, 'cause I gotta tell you, boy, where you're heading, your little nuggets are going to be fresh meat. They will all want a piece of you." Yeah, he's starting to shake.

"You threatening me, cop?" he says while smirking. I see him, though, his throat starting to bob, voice starting to quiver. Won't be long now before he's bending, breaking, and signing the sweet tune called snitch. There isn't a lawyer in all this country who will get him bail. Not with all the cocaine, crack, and speeders this kid had on him.

"I don't have to threaten, boy. Not when my promises are worth gold around here," I snarl, grab his hand, and bend his pinky finger back until it snaps, crackles, and fucking pops. Shit, that had to hurt.

"You crazy fuck! You'll lose your badge for that," he screams, voice sounding as if he hasn't reached puberty yet. Shit, the boy doesn't even have a set of balls big enough to wail like that. It's still echoing off these walls. Pussy.

"That's right, buddy; you better loosen up those vocal chords, because soon enough, you'll be someone's screaming little bitch. Now, where were we?" I take hold of his wrist and bend it back. Place a foot on the top of his and press. I'm pushing my limits here. I really do not give a fuck. "I could do this all day, you know? Break fingers and toes. Tell me something, Richie Rich, you ever been punched in your Adam's apple? Do you have any idea what that does to a man?" I ask, draw my other arm back, internally laughing when he tries to jerk free in order to bring his hands up to cover his neck only to remember they're cuffed to the arm of the chair.

"You're violating my rights," he spits.

"You lost any rights you had when you starting selling drugs, you little piss ant. Now, back to my question. Do you know what it feels like?"

"Fuck you."

"I'll pass. Your type of pussy isn't my style. Let me tell you what it does. It could crush your windpipe. Make it hard to breathe, and that isn't the worst part." I literally cringe remembering all too well being struck there during a training exercise in the academy. The worst physical pain I've felt in my life. I couldn't breathe or see for five minutes. I seriously thought I was going to die. "The impact to your throat is horrible, man. Depending on how you get hit, it could crush your windpipe. It turns the blood in your veins to red hot liquid and courses straight to your balls. It ignites this burning, incapacitating pain that feels like hell and sets your midsection on fire. You can't swallow, can't breathe, and can't get your balls or your Adam's apple out of the back of your throat. In other words, it fucking hurts."

"I'll take it from here, Corelli." Agent Dietrich of the FBI waltzes into the room, slamming the door behind him. It's about damn time he joined in. He can have this scum-sucking motherfucker. Gladly.

"You've either been saved or sentenced to death, boy. He's ten times worse than I am." I keep my stare steady on this twenty-something-year-old kid. His life is gone before he has the chance to properly get his dick wet. Too bad he got stuck with me priming him and Dietrich to finish. He isn't going to see pussy for a long time. Dumb-ass punk.

"Get this little shit out of my precinct," I voice, turn around without another word, and slam the door behind me. I'm not in the mood to deal with fucking idiots today. Selfish piece of shit.

I take a few steps down the hall, round the corner, and rest my back against the wall, letting it support me. I don't know how much more of this I can take. The pretending that I don't give a fuck about anything when the truth is it's all killing me. It's as if someone has gutted me open and pulled out everything inside of me that makes me want to care. Pure fucking agony, and I can't seem to hold on to it tightly enough anymore. I'm hollowed the fuck out. Bone dry. And if I don't get it together, one of the only things I do care about is going to be gone. My job.

I left here a few months ago to try and get my head on straight. To find some sort of peace with the woman who wrecked my life. Who stole my soul the day she left me at the altar. She left an empty hole in my chest that has now rotted out, and here I stand with my hands clenched to my sides, my pulse in my throat, living a life without meaning. Life without her and no peace in sight.

She should be in my life. Our time together should be flashing before my eyes with untainted memories. Beautiful ones. A family. Instead, this entire situation is so fucked up that never in my wildest thoughts would I have imagined seeing her again would drudge up old wounds that I thought I'd buried. One of them the unexpected reason she left me. "Fucking hell. I need to drag myself out of this," I announce to myself. I'm spiraling out of control. Worse than I've ever been.

When I left, I prayed she would be gone when I returned. That my words of not wanting anything to do with her would sink in and she would have relented and disappeared again. No such luck. She's still here and still fucking with my head, my heart, and everything else. I can't get her out of my system, and it's driving me back to a time in my life I can't handle going back to. I'm barely hanging on to the last shred of sanity I have left.

Hell, I didn't even want to come back. The truth is, I had to no matter how much it ripped at my soul. Time got away from me, and before I knew it, I was headed back here for Riddick and Cora's wedding. I had to be there for him and for the woman he thought had died, only to find her very much alive. The man has been there for me more times than I care to count. More drunken random nights that big fucker has saved my ass from doing something stupid, and even though I've avoided every wedding since my own never happened, I came back for him. For Cora and Ethan.

It took me less than a minute to feel her presence as we all watched Ron escort Cora down the aisle. I looked up, and there Lynne was, standing on her porch watching them begin to exchange their vows while staring at me. It took everything I had not to march my ass across the sand and knock some sense into her. To cut out her heart in the same way she did mine. To choke the living shit out of her until she begged me to stop. I should have done it then, and I should do it now. Except, as much as I hate to admit, I can't do to her what she did to me. Especially when deep down inside I know the reason why she left.

That's only part of the reason my head is all fucked up. Now, Jude and Vivian are engaged. Happy and living together with Theo, the young boy Jude adopted, and their crazy-ass dogs.

I'm not angry that my two best friends are happy while I'm over here wallowing in my self-pity. They deserve happiness. The truth is, I'm pissed off because she's still here. She should have been my happiness. She's everywhere I don't want or need her to be, and why the fuck Lynne Chapman has come back to stir up memories I don't want to remember is beyond me.

It's been more years than I care to count, and yet I still can't get Lynne out of my head, out of my mind, or out of my heart. I've tried. God, how I've tried to shake that woman loose from my life, to pretend she never existed, and yet for some fucked-up reason I can't. If a shrink were to analyze my way of trying to forget her, I'm sure I'd be locked up for life, sent to a deserted island reserved for the crazies, or told that killing, fucking, and drinking only leads to more self-destruction. Maybe I should make an appointment with her. She is a psychologist after all. Doesn't fucking matter. The bomb inside of me ignited too long ago to try and disengage the fucker now. The funny thing is, it took all these years to finally blow up, and I don't have a clue how to mend the fragmented pieces.

"Tyson, what the fuck, brother." Jude grips hold of my shoulders before I slump forward to the floor.

"I can't fucking do this anymore," I wheeze out, look him stone-cold dead in the eyes for several beats before his intense, worried gaze becomes too much for me to take. Fuck, I want to tell him what the hell is going on so bad. It's one of those stories where you have no idea where to begin because you can't quite figure it out yourself. I've only held it in for years, ever since we all returned from the desert where we served our country. Christ, the memories flood in like a tsunami. I'm drowning. Damn near gasping for air.

"Something tells me you aren't talking about being the best at beating a suspect down, man," he gives way to revealing how well he knows me.

"That shit is easy. I have his ass all geared up for the FBI. He'll talk." I've been down this road with Jude before, as many times as I have with Riddick. They want me to tell them why I meant so little to the woman I thought I would spend the rest of my life with. They have no clue that her reason for leaving me is what has me so fucked up in my head that I can't see straight. Well, maybe they do; they've just given me the time and space I've needed all this time. There isn't any amount of time or space that will fix this. The only way to do it is to talk it out with her, and I don't think I can do it without wanting to kill someone over it. Starting with her good-for-nothing parents.

For years, I suspected it had to do with her father hating my guts. He never thought I was good enough for his precious little girl. Kind of ironic when he didn't pay her a lick of attention himself.

I was the poor young kid whose mother died when he was five, leaving a heartbroken husband behind who took to the bottle and then took his hands to his son. He beat me until the day came along where all that alcohol snuck up on his piss-poor excuse of a parent's ass and turned his liver as dark as his black heart and killed him. I hope he's rotting in hell.

Fucking bastards. Both her father and mine.

Then my mind twisted around itself again. I thought there was no way in hell she would allow him to change her mind. She hated him and everything he represented. His cheating ways. His lying and deceptive behavior. Lynne wanted away from him and the lifestyle she led. The fakeness behind being rich when money meant nothing to her. She had proven that tenfold by falling in love with me.

Then there was the it-must-have-been-another-man phase. But I quickly tossed that notion in the trash right alongside my bleeding heart. She wasn't a cheater. Not with the way her heart broke whenever she thought of her mother and how she cut a blind eye to her dad's philandering ways.

Her mother is a cold-hearted bitch. I don't do cheating. That shit doesn't sit well with me at all. That woman, though, she deserves everything that is placed in her lap.

The entire time I fought next to my brothers, I wondered what it was I had done to make the only woman I loved kill my chance at ever finding peace. I rarely spoke of it to anyone. It came out in my dreams, in my nightmares, and with every bullet I barreled into the enemy's skull. I hated her, and I loved her. Still do. And that right there is the biggest issue that's fucking with my head. It's me pulling the trigger, and the bullet remains lodged in my skull. Keeping me alive when all I want to do is die.

"Go home. I'll cover your ass," Jude snaps me out of my heartbreaking memories.

"Thanks. I'll call you later." I push off the wall, hesitate in my steps to tell him more before exhaling a deep breath, shoving open the side door, and striding over to my bike without giving him the truth so he'll stop worrying about me. "Someday, man," I whisper, gear myself up, and hit the open road toward my apartment.

Ten minutes later, I'm forcing my way through my door. The loneliness is striking me hard as I take in the bare white walls, the lack of furniture, and a television that takes up half of one of the walls. I despise this place. It's quiet, subdued, and has never felt like home. Nothing has since her.

"Goddamn it!" I roar, toss my helmet on the well-worn leather couch, and make my way into the kitchen, where I pull down a bottle of whiskey out of the cupboard, grab a cigar, and open the slider that leads to the deck. "Why is she doing this to me?" I take several swigs, place the bottle on the table, and light up. The gray-blue smoke starts filtering through the dusk-filled evening air.

All I can see is her. She went from a young woman who was growing into womanhood to a goddess with thick, heavy, brown hair with streaks of blond that rests upon her shoulders, soft full lips on that mouth that always drove me out of my mind, and a sharp tongue. Toned arms and legs. Striking. The object of my dreams or the demise that puts me one step further to hell.

Every curve on her sinful body appears to be a handful. The slant of her haunting green eyes is clear as a bell right now. The rise of her ample chest is still humming through my veins, and I hate myself for allowing her to sit stagnantly, to take up space that doesn't belong to her anymore. *You sure about that?* Fucking positive.

When I first noticed it was her on the beach all those months ago, I thought I had lost my mind. Time warped me back to the heartbroken young man who lost his mother, his father, and then the only woman he's ever allowed in. A broken man split right down the middle. One half man, one half a complete stranger. I have no clue who Tyson Corelli is anymore.

Which was why seeing her that day, her long goddess-like legs taking small, tentative steps my way, was worse than anything I could have imagined. I pictured her walking to me in her wedding dress, and when reality sunk in and she was standing before me in a white, short, sleeveless dress instead, her face as innocent-looking as the day we met, I lost my shit. A neurotic drug pumped hard through my veins. Life's dirty lesson she taught me pounded in my ears and every short hair at the nape of my neck poked out.

I had torn into her before she had a chance to speak. I yelled over the roar of the sea. My throat burned, and for the first time in my life, I wished to the Almighty God I was having one of my nightmares. Except I wasn't. Lynne Chapman was a vision standing before me. Eyes misted over, tears streaming down her delicate face. I wanted to kiss her, bruise her lips, and cry.

"What in the ever-loving fuck are you doing here?" I'd said, lifting one hand and pointing a finger in her face.

"I came here for you. You need to let me explain," she begged, and

my head jerked back. What in the actual fuck?

"*I need to let you explain? You don't worry about my Goddamn needs. Now, get the hell off this beach and away from me. Besides, an explanation should have come the next day, the next month. Hell, a year later. Not after well over a decade. I don't want an explanation. I know the truth. I've known for years, Lynne.*" *Her face turned as white as her dress. Her tears dried up instantly and her mouth went slack. She's beautiful, and I needed her gone.*

"*How do you know?*" *she had asked. Confusion dripping off her and blending with the waves. I could have taunted and teased her. Made her wonder, but I didn't. I was in shock over seeing her while standing in a spot I loved more than anything. The beach. And here she was sharing my air, making me breathe her in, and for the first time in years destroying the only place I found solace in allowing my thoughts to escape me. It was the only time I did not want to be standing where I was, gazing out into the water and thinking about how much of my life I allowed her to piss away. She was standing too close. Her smell surrounded me. I wanted to touch her, choke her, and for one damn minute, fuck her and taste her. Until reality settled in and my anger took over.*

"*How do I know? Let's call it life's lesson as to finding out why my fiancée didn't have the guts to face me on our wedding day. To tell me to my face that she didn't love me enough to become my wife. That the woman I loved didn't trust in our love enough to believe that a man and woman fight through life together. Call it whatever you want, Lynne. I don't care.*" *I couldn't stand to be there anymore. Her explanation as to why she had suddenly landed in my friend's backyard didn't matter. I called after the dogs, turned to leave, and her last words teaching me that life had another brick wall for me to slam into broke me.*

"*I had to do it. You deserved more,*" *she whispered.*

"*I deserved the truth. I deserved you. So, fuck you and everyone else who kept this from me. You didn't love me enough to let me be the one to help you.*"

"*I loved you enough to let you go. I still love you.*"

CHAPTER TWO

LYNNE

"I don't care how it appears, mother. I'm not doing it." My God, I should have asked my therapist years ago to please explain to me how I have the same blood running through my veins as her and my father. I resemble the two of them about as much as absence and presence go together. Which, when it comes to me, the two of them identify better than anyone how vaguely absent my presence has been in their lives for years. They care about themselves. Their appearances. The high-quality communication with the same type of people as them. Liars. Cheaters. Manipulators. Public figures. While me, I've lived that life and hated every moment of it.

"Oh, for heaven's sake, Lynne. It's one small ribbon-cutting ceremony. After everything we've done for you over these past years, it's the least you can do." I pull my cell phone from my ear, staring at the device as if I've just pulled a cackling hyena out of the side of my head. She's crazy. Poisonous too. Bitch.

"Excuse me," I say, befuddled. I should ask her if she needs a session with me. I'd make her pay, and it wouldn't be with money. It would be with my fist upside her head. "And what precisely have you done for me, mother?" Besides brainwash me into believing true love doesn't exist. Oh, and let's not forget that by doing so you've killed my soul in the process." *Here it comes. The chalkboard fingernail screeching.*

I pull the phone away from my ear before I go deaf. "My God, girl;

we've done everything for you. Why are you so disrespectful to me? You weren't raised this way. Let me guess; it has to do with Tyson, doesn't it. You're back with him. You will never learn. For Christ's sakes, Lynne." God, I hate her. I really do, and that is a horrible thing to say about your mother.

The sting from hearing his name bitterly once again slices through me. I can imagine the sparks going off in her brain. I wish they would fry her skull. Turn it into ashes. She's playing connect the dots when there is nothing but a blank piece of paper to work with. She's going to bitch and moan about the damage he caused to their house. Or how he's still not good enough for me, or the best one of them all, how a man like him will never stand by my side once he knows the truth. The same way she thinks my ex-husband did. Except she's wrong. Robert knew before we married; it was me who pulled away from him after five years of pretending I loved him. Of trying to forget a face that whispered my name whenever I thought about him. It was daily. Nightly. And every time Robert touched me I wished it were Tyson.

I couldn't live that way anymore. The truth was slowly eating me from the inside out, carving a painful, permanent scar onto my soul. I was crucifying myself. Killing a man who deserved more out of life. Slowly dying in a faraway place I had no help to claw out of because of them. They put me there. Left me to rot in my own poisonous well of guilt. *I hate them.*

Marrying someone else was the one way I conjured up in my mind that I could lay my biggest mistake to rest. To try and somehow stop beating myself up. I cared about Robert, but I never loved him. Not in a way a wife should love her husband. He wasn't him. The only person who accepted me for the woman I was. Tyson would have been there for me. I know he would have, and yet I someone went along with listening to her and my father. It won't matter if someday I learn to forgive myself; I will never forgive them for putting the doubt in my head in the first place.

My brain kept playing teeter-totter with my heart. One day, I thought it was best to let him go, the next, I wanted to tell him everything, to let him make up his own mind. In the end, my head won and my heart was nowhere to be found.

I knew I lost Tyson the day I left him with a simple note. Telling him we were too young to get married and I had cold feet. Wanted to explore the world. Nothing but lies. Too many of them covered up by my parents. No one knows more than me how shameful I feel. It's unforgiving.

Only it really wasn't covered up at all. Somehow, Tyson found out, and now I'm staying in this town to do whatever it takes to get him to listen to me. I just need him to hear me out.

"I'm not discussing this with you. This is your final warning, mother. If you do not stop talking about him as if you are better than he is, then you may as well consider yourself the parent of two daughters instead of three, because I am done. On second thought, I'm done anyway." I hang up on her before she tries to get the last word in. *Trolling conniver.*

"Thank you for believing I can succeed on my own, mother. I should have disowned everyone in your perfect little family years ago. Starting today, you and my father will no longer be a part of my life," I pledge to the walls of my new office. Toss my phone on the desk and spin my chair to stare out the window. All they want is to see their faces in the paper. To pretend we're the perfect family when we are anything but.

She knows better than to pull this bullshit on me. I've warned them all when I first moved here to back the hell off. They still think they can mark me, break me until I have nothing left. If I didn't hate them as much as I do, I would pity them for being my victims for years. They taught me well.

My darling mother, Ellen Chapman, has dealt her last hand when it comes to being a casualty in her made-up world with her fake marriage to an even phonier man. Now she's his messenger, dishing out demands to the only one of his three daughters who could give a shit how a person's image looks to anyone but those who live in their illusional world. Los Angeles. The fictitious city of angels, my ass. More like the city of the devil and his willing advocates.

While my sisters, Larissa and Laney, are both married to high-profile attorneys who work for my father and follow in the footsteps of the high and mighty prestigious LA circle of the who's who, I simply couldn't care less. Fuck them all.

I care about my sisters, and we get along, as long as I pretend to play by the rules. Which I don't. Not anymore.

It's going to kill me to lose my sisters. I would never put them in the middle of any of this. They'll choose on their own. And as much as it pains me to admit, it won't be the right side. *They've chosen already, Lynne. Were they there for you when your world ended? No, they were not.*

They know not to bring up my past or the pain that slices away at my heart over the mess I've made of my life. They've simply chosen to ignore it. Live in the same circular bubble. Not my parents, though. I really don't think the two of them know the meaning of letting shit go or showing their love. Hell, I don't think it's in their vocabulary or their blood.

Things were somewhat different when I was a child. They were half-way decent parents. I never got the 'I love you' or bedtime stories. At least not that I can remember. They simply left me alone.

I always felt like the odd daughter. The black sheep. The only daughter without a purpose in life. Boring, as my father would say. Although my parents doted on my sisters more than they did me, I respected them as much as a child could. It all went to hell when I showed up at our house with Tyson. Good old Richard and Ellen Chapman displayed who they really were. They hated him, and in return, I grew to hate them back. I rebelled against them. Snuck out and dated him anyway. Fell completely in love. And I've loved him since.

I was shocked they agreed to pay for my wedding when I told them we were getting married with or without their help. Of course, they didn't agree out of their happiness for me. It was all for show. For them. Always about them.

"Men are bastards," my mother would always say. "They can never be faithful or stay true to their marriage vows." At first, I listened to her rant, but not once did I believe Tyson was like that. He loved me. And then my world fell apart. My life wilted, and somehow, I started to believe her because I was young and in shock over the news that was delivered to me a few weeks before Tyson and I were to be married.

All I could think about was ruining a man's life. It had nothing to do with him ruining mine. How his dreams would be shredded. His life destroyed and mine shattering over watching him fall because of me.

The lies I'd been fed barely skimmed under the radar separating me from hell. They were big, so big that once I came out of my shell and sought out some heart-wrenching truths, I couldn't believe my parents could do this to me. To him. Destroying lives while sheltering themselves from a conspiratorial theory that blew my mind. *They shattered me.*

My father was ten times worse than my mother. If I didn't know better, I would swear to this day that man prayed for something horrible to happen to make Tyson disappear from my life. He never thought he was good enough for me. Never thought we could make it on a soldier's salary. Never thought he would hold my hand through the pain. It's ironic to say my father never once held it, either.

It wasn't until a few years later when I started college at Yale that I came to the conclusion my news would have destroyed Tyson in the way of worry, fear, and the unknown, instead of the way both of my parents had convinced me of. I grew to despise them both after that. I became cold. Detached. And when they would call me out on it, I explained that after two years of living in darkness, being behind in my education that I deserved to spread my wings, to be on my own. Except, just like them, I learned to use people to my advantage and I needed them to pay for ten years of college, so I could sit in this laid-back office with my degree in psychology. So, I pretended to be fine. Flew back from Connecticut for the holidays as often as I could. Met Robert my sophomore year of college, married him a year later with the finest of fine in attendance. Wore the fancy ball gowns at charity events all the while hating every minute I had to spend with the two of them. I kept it all inside. And now, I don't have to tolerate their shit anymore. I can tell them to fuck right off. To kiss my ass and stay away from me.

I've known Tyson's whereabouts for years now. Ever since I gained the nerve to look him up. I had to. The not knowing was eating me alive. I lost track of him the day I let him go. I lost myself, too.

Not only did the pain make a reappearance in my soul the day I found out he lived in Santa Barbara, only a few hours from the place I had escaped from, but it also destroyed me all over again. It also completed an already crumbling marriage, a relationship built on lies. I simply did not know how to go on. Robert is a wonderful man. He didn't deserve the hell I put him through. He took it like a champ, though. Told me we both deserved happiness and to go out and find mine. It's only taken me several years to do so.

"Lynne," my secretary Maggie interrupts my thoughts. I turn around to face the fifty-one-year-old woman who's not only my secretary; she's my only friend in this town. Maggie lives across the street from me. We met on the beach a few days after I moved in. Became friends instantly when she asked if I minded she brought her two young grandsons over to swim and play on my little strip of the beach. I adore her. She's the mother I've always wished for. A confidante who knows everything about me in the short span of our irreplaceable relationship.

"I'm sorry, Maggie. I just hung up with my mother. I'll come help you finish putting things away." I prepare to stand only to have her lean over my desk with a concerned look on her face.

"It's not that. I'm finished," she whispers.

"Well, that was fast. Is everything okay?" I enquire. She's scaring me a little by the intense way her shoulders stiffen and her eyes glare at me as if she expects me to read her mind.

"Jude Westbrooke is in the reception area. He's demanding to speak with you." My eyes go wide, and I gulp. Jude is my neighbor. He, like his girlfriend, his son, and all the rest of Tyson's friends avoid me like the black cloaks of death whenever they see me. I haven't spoken to the man since I tried to help them when some crazy stalker tried to hurt them. I left shortly after that. Went to stay with my sister Larissa in LA for a few weeks. I didn't stay for her. I wanted to spend time with my ten-year-old niece, Elizabeth. I then moved into a hotel across town. Remained busy with contractors on remodeling the building I bought for my office. I avoided going back to my new home to stay until I heard Tyson was back. It's amazing the things you hear while sitting on your porch or balcony with our houses being close enough together. I overheard Jude and Vivian talking about how Tyson had better have his ass back for Riddick's wedding. I waited until the day before to spend the night there. I hid and watched for him.

Tyson's lips moved a mile a minute that very same day I left when he said he wanted nothing to do with me. However, his eyes…The ones I have memorized by heart. The ones I can count every tiny golden fleck mixed in with the deep, dark mossy green of his irises told an entirely different story. The man is gutted in the same way as I am. Probably more.

"Send him in," I bite out. Not directing my negative tone toward her. I'm sure she knows why he's here right now and it's not a neighborly visit. He wants to know what's going on.

Well, I have news for him. He's not getting anything out of me. Not until I talk to Tyson and explain that at the time, I thought I was giving him a chance to live a life without me being a burden to him. How wrong I was about it all. It's a life neither one of us can get back. I have no doubt in my mind that is why Jude has shown up here. He wants me to leave and to never come back. He's in for one hell of a rude awakening. I'm tired of backing down and showing weakness. Whatever he has to say is nothing compared to the hell I've been through and survived. He can screw off like the rest of them.

"Alright. Just know I'm right outside if you need me. I like Jude. He's been nothing but kind to me. However, I'm not afraid to put that man in his place. You stand your ground, do you hear me?" she says, voice carrying loud enough I'm sure he heard her.

"You know I will," I reassure her with all the confidence in the world. My insides shake as she walks out with a warm breeze only to be replaced by the freezing chills and Jude's ice-cold stare. He shuts the door behind him, stands firmly in place, and stares me down.

"That intimidating look may work well on the criminals you pick up; I assure you, Jude, it will not work on me. Now, what can I help you with?" Yes, I know that Tyson and his friends are cops. I know everything there is to know about him. He left as planned for the Army shortly after I left him. He's a womanizer. Sleeps around, drinks, and gets into fights. He's angry, bitter, and out of control, and it all reflects on me. I've studied the symptoms of a broken person. I'm one myself.

I know very little about his time at war. I'm sure some of his anger stems from there. I feared for his life every day. Kept up with the news while terror weighed on my shoulders every second he was deployed. I'm so proud of him for what he's done with his life. Growing from a young kid with the odds of turning into a criminal stacked against him to a man of honor. A soldier turned cop. I couldn't ask for a better man than him.

I still haven't been able to let him go. The man I left lives in the tattered mess of my heart, and I never stopped praying our lives would have been different, that fate wouldn't have snuck up on me and kicked my feet right out from under me. Stole our chance at happiness. I've loved Tyson since the first day I laid my eyes on him. Through time and therapy, I thought I would be able to stop loving him. That there was no way love could be this strong that months, years, and a decade later it would still linger. The precious memories I kept locked away swarmed to the forefront of my mind the minute I saw him again. Stolen kisses, bodies tangled together. Our hearts so full of promises to one another. I broke them all. Broke him. Broke me. I'm here to fix it. Somehow.

I remain calm, matching Jude's gaze while every cell in my body is a quivering mess. My stomach shifts uneasily and sweat breaks out at the nape of my neck. But I will not falter or allow him to see that his presence is terrifying me.

"When Tyson first told me it was you, I didn't want to believe it. I prayed for you to disappear, to crawl back under your rock and stay the hell away from him. Now, after seeing what this is doing to him, I've changed my mind. Before I get into why I think you owe me an explanation as to what your plans are, I want you to know I'm standing here not trying to intimidate you. I'm here to tell you if your reasons are not legit, I will fucking destroy you." Good luck. You can't destroy something that's already broken.

"I don't owe you a damn thing," I snarl. My tone is condescending to my own ears. How dare he waltz in here and demand things of me when I tried to be kind, only to have their noses shoved in the air the minute they found out who I was. I understand why they are all acting as if I don't exist. The way they all ignored me the night Riddick and Cora were married. They knew I was standing there watching, my eyes glued to the man in the dark gray suit, the lavender tie, and wishing I were there with him. I loved how his dark eyes glistened with the last rays of sunlight angling across his rugged face. The way he slicked back his dark blond hair. The way every step he took on that sandy beach showed off his toned, thick, muscular thighs. His jacket stretched across mountainous planes of muscle on his arms, his back, and down to a rock-hard ass. I loved it all. All except the fact he avoided my stare. Refused to acknowledge my existence.

My words of asking him what this is doing to Tyson are lodged in my throat. Jude isn't going to give me an answer any more than I'm going to give him one. It's none of his business as far as I'm concerned.

"That's where you are dead fucking wrong. Tyson is a mess. You being here is fucking with his head, and now it's screwing with his job. He's my friend, my brother, and you've hurt him enough. Either you get on with whatever the hell you have planned, or you make it known that you'll stay the hell away from him, or so help me God, Lynne."

"So, help you God, what?" I stand, place my hands on my desk, and lean forward. "You'll drive me out of town? Destroy my reputation? Arrest me? I don't scare that easily, Jude. There isn't a damn thing you can do or say to me that will make me run. It's too late for forgiveness, and I know it. I'm not here to hurt him, and frankly, I really don't give a shit if you believe me or not. He hasn't told you a thing, has he?" I'm playing with fire and spitting it in a circle around his feet. It's a dangerous game to play, and I really don't care what this smug man thinks of me. I stopped caring about anything except Tyson years ago. Jude and his big bad self can't hurt me any more than I've hurt myself.

I'm taken aback with myself, too. I've never stood up to anyone like this before. It must be the day to defend myself.

"No, he hasn't. For some ungodly reason, he's protecting you. What is it? Did you cheat on him? Have his baby and put it for adoption?" Oh God, help me. Something inside of me just shattered.

"Get out." I raise my voice, my body starting to shake profusely. "How dare you come in here and speak to me that way. You don't know a thing." My voice is breaking. I need him out of here before I crumble to the floor. He's getting warmer to the truth, and it's breaking me wide open. He can't see me this way. Dissecting me behind his glasses. Not until I've told Tyson everything.

"I never cheated on him, and if I were ever to have been fortunate enough to be the mother of his child, I would never give him or her away. Please go," I say, the chords in my throat straining to keep the strings that hold my voice box from going taut and exposing a high pitch that would shatter glass.

I can't hold back the ache inside of me any longer. Tears begin to fall. My emotions are cracking and crumbling. He's protecting me by not telling them. Why? There's nothing to protect. It's not his problem. I made sure of it when I left. To him, it should mean nothing.

I sit down before my legs give out. The tears start turning to sobs, burning my eyes, plugging up my nose. I close them, so I don't have to watch this man gloat. To see the look of satisfaction on his face in knowing he's broken me. God, how I wish I would have done things differently, that I would have trusted my heart and told Tyson what was going on. I knew I demolished him and I'm doing it all over again. I just can't walk away. Not this time.

"Here." I still at the softness of Jude's voice, open my tightly pinched eyes, and take the box of tissues he hands me. "I apologize for making you upset. I really do. I'm worried about him, and you're the one with all the answers. I guess what I'm trying to say is, please do something. Whatever is going on is killing him." God, his plea is destroying me. It's surfacing every memory I've tried to bury.

"Where is he?"

CHAPTER THREE

TYSON

A soft knock on my door wakes me from my slumbering sleep. Rubbing the back of my stiff neck and pushing up from the couch, I reach for the light on the table, flick it on, and let my eyes adjust.

"Goddamn, that burns." I thunder out a few more explicit curse words and press the heels of my palms into my eyes. I need to focus. Remain sane and pull the knife out of my bleeding heart.

I remained on my deck for the longest time thinking and remembering for I don't know how long, tossing back the golden-brown liquid until I grew tired, my heart aching as I allowed my mind to drift to my past, slamming time and time again to the ground below me. The air outside became so thick I could have vanished in it. My head ready to pop off my neck with all the stress on my troubled mind. All this wear and tear on my body has got to stop. Especially over her. A woman who didn't love me enough to let me be the one to help her.

The knock comes again. Louder this time. I can feel their impatience with every throbbing thud on the thick piece of steel. Fucking Jude or Riddick. Those two need to back the hell off and give me the space I need. They left me alone while I was gone, but now they are climbing all over my ass. The unanswered text messages and voice messages over the past several hours are proof of it. "Well, get your shit together, asshole, and then they won't," I mumble, grab my t-shirt, and hoist myself up to answer the door.

"I'm coming, you motherfucker," I grumble, swing open the door, and sober up instantly when I see who's on the other side. A sharp jab of the knife pushes in further. I'm staring into a gaze that massacres me. Her expression is strong-minded. While mine, it has to be screaming with a vengeance shadowed in doubt. *What in the hell is she doing here?*

"Hello, Tyson," Lynne says softly, her face a vision. I can't seem to put my thoughts into words at how beautiful she is. They stumble around in my head, spin out of control, and I suck in a breath at the fact she is standing at my door. Her curvy, slender body delicate yet strong and powerful with the way she holds her head up high, her shoulders back, and those light green eyes she always claimed were darker than mine are seizing and swirling with a hundred different bleeding raw emotions. Anger compresses against my tongue. It sharpens, seizes hold, and breaks past my parched lips.

"What the fuck are you doing here? I thought I made myself clear when I said I wanted you gone and out of my life?" Slash. I hope that stung. Burned. Bled. *It hurts, doesn't it?*

I don't know what the hell I truly want right now. My mind is fucked up more than ever now that she's here. This woman has me caught in a web. A deadly spider ready to bite, and here I stand welcoming the fucking venom to seep into my veins. *Slam the Goddamn door in her face.* I can't.

"I promise I'll stay as far away from you as I can if you'll let me explain. You ran away from me on the beach. I'm begging you to hear me out. Please, Tyson." Sweet God. Even with her face pinched up, her lips quivering, she is hands down the most gorgeous woman I have ever seen. I'm slowly dying. It's painful, heartburning, and if I allow her into my home, only God knows what I will end up doing. *You do nothing.*

"Why in the ever-loving fuck would I listen to a word you have to say? You promised a lot of things you never followed through with, Lynne. Your word means shit to me," I say on the fly. It's the truth, and she knows it. *How does it feel to have a knife plunged straight into your chest?*

And quit fucking looking at me like that. Here gaze is traveling up and down my chest. Across my shoulders, my neck, and lands on my lips.

"I know I can't ask you to forgive me. I'm asking you to try and understand." Her voice creaks and agony spills from her mouth. God, I'm tired of this. The hurting, the hate. All the pain that dominates inside of my chest. I want it gone.

"Fuck," I snarl out. Pull my shirt over my head and gesture for her to come in. I'm going to regret this. My past is at my door, assaulting me back to a time where I had my life together only to watch it be ruined in a matter of hours. I haven't been the same man since.

Familiarity hits me when her smell assaults my nose. Slightly sharp, flowery, and sexy as fucking hell. She walks past me on those long, long legs to sit on the couch. My dick jumps. The poor bastard hasn't seen any action since she waltzed into my life again, and up until now, I've refused to jack him off to her face, her body, her deliciously intoxicating mind that can't seem to disconnect. Seeing her now with her tight ass, her tits, and her entire being in my space has me wishing to God I would have done something to ease the pain going down my spine. She's fucking me every which she can except the one way my body craves her to.

I take her in while she studies my empty apartment. Sighing as she looks at the bare walls, the empty place I call home. She's vague as she stares down my hollow home. *Welcome to my fucking life, sweetheart.* It's all you're doing. Dull. Dead. Empty.

"Could you sit down, please?" she asks, hands wringing in her lap.

"No, I won't. This isn't going to be one of your therapy sessions. I'm beyond getting anyone's help." Her lips tremble in a steady, fast beat before she bows her head with shame written all over it. Goddamn it. I should have never said that. I didn't mean it the way it sounded.

It's obvious by the way her face has turned white she went to counseling after what happened to her. My heart swings back and forth regretfully in my chest. A slow and heavy pendulum. I do feel for her and everything she's been through. I visualized it many times over the years in my head. The heartache and pain she must have endured. The probability of being alone in a fucked-up situation.

"Did you know that talking with my own therapist is what made the decision for me to become one? She helped me so much. Made me realize that what happened to me was out of my control. It was life's plan for me all along. I want to do the same for others," she murmurs, and fuck all if I don't feel that tweak my heart. A pit of despair. For her. God help me.

"I didn't." My answer is short, it's harsh, and if she doesn't get on with this, I'm asking her to leave. I can't do this. I'm stroking out. Swimming in an endless sea, drifting further away from shore. My death.

"Right. Well, here goes. I woke up excited to be going to the doctor to get on the pill, as you were aware. No more condoms. It was going to be the perfect wedding night. Just me and you and nothing in between. Laney thought I was crazy for being all giddy over some strange woman looking at me. The doctor ran all kinds of tests. Gave me my pills and I left. Two days later, they called me back in. I had no idea what was going on or what to do, so I told my parents. They both insisted on going with me. I've regretted every day for not telling you first. For not having you go with me instead. Things may or may not be different if I did, I don't know. The only thing I know for sure is, it would have saved you the pain from the lie I told. You would have known the truth and made the decision yourself." She pauses, and I need a drink.

The problem with that is, I can't move. Hearing this from her after all this time is going to dull the hate I have for her. It's going to fuck me up and tear me down. A part of me wants to stop her, tell her I can't hear anymore, while the other part, the one that's beating sense into my head, is telling me she deserves to get this out. I see clearly the woman she is; she's tough. Any woman who has been shredded raw the way she was at such a young age and still holds her head high is as strong as a person can be.

"Anyway, by the time we got there, the doctor's office had been cleared out. No patients, no secretary. Just Doctor McGlone and her nurse. To this day, I think my father called and somehow found out before I did. I had cancer, Tyson. An eighteen-year-old woman diagnosed with ovarian cancer. I was devastated. All I kept thinking about was you and all the talks we had about how once we were settled in life that we would start a family. Those two weeks before our wedding left me wilting away, while my father, he demanded more tests. He hired specialists to come to our home. Snuck me into the hospital to see the best doctors, and each one of them told me the same thing. If I didn't have a full hysterectomy, I would die. The cancer would spread and kill me. All I wanted to do was curl up in your arms and have you tell me everything would be alright. That you and I would make it through this." I stand there. A stone-cold statue. Condensing everything she exposed into summarization while her misery covers me like a cape full of sharp-pointed daggers I never expected. It's molding to my skin, squeezing my lungs, assaulting me, and awakening parts of my body that have been dead for years.

"You were young, naïve, and I'm sorry this happened to you. I truly am. You're right in saying you took a choice away from me that was mine to make. A choice I'll never get back. I loved you so much, and I know you loved me; you wouldn't have shut me out the way you did if you weren't convinced that I would have regretted it at some point. I would have stood by your side, held your hand, and we would have fought all of it together. Your parents took your illness and twisted it to their advantage, didn't they? They talked you out of telling me. Convinced you to not follow through with a promise you made to be my wife. They hated me from day one. Constantly saying you were young, that you could do better, and that I wouldn't be able to provide for you. To live up to their standards. Did you know I tore that town apart searching for you? I threatened your parents, your sisters. The staff. Everyone. You simply vanished, and they forced you to do it." I point my finger in her direction out of the anger consuming me for her parents. They did this to us, and she let them.

She has no idea how much I want to jab my finger in her chest. To make her feel the agony forcing its way out from my shredded flesh. I breathe in deeply, my lungs expanding to full capacity over divulging this stored-up information. I'm barely breathing. Floating on wobbly legs to keep me from falling.

I lift my brows, leveling my eyes with hers in a hard challenge. I could stand here and tell her how her father had me cuffed and threatened to arrest me. I could tell her that her mother spit in my face. Told me that the entire time we were planning our small, intimate wedding, she was wearing a mask of happiness over her face. Pretending to be ecstatic for her daughter. Except I won't do that to her. I'm a man of honor, not a callous fucker out to hurt her any more than she has been.

Lynne is a smart woman. Blinded by the control of an evil man and his corrupted wife. She knows they did, and I won't consider trying to forgive her until she admits it.

"They're the ones who talked me into going to Mercy Hospital in Baltimore for my surgery. I wanted to tell you. I swear I did." My face is burning with anger. She's poking around the truth. Not spilling out what I want to hear. What I deserve.

She hated them. The things I want to say to her about them she knew. We never kept a thing from each other, so why is she beating around a bush that's been burned down for years?

"Goddamn it, Lynne. Quit protecting them. Jesus Christ. You're not a young woman anymore. Tell me." She jumps at my command. Her lips start trembling, and her body begins to shake. I should feel elated over making her feel whatever agony she is feeling. I don't. Still, it's something I have every right to hear from her. I'll seek my revenge for them when I'm done untangling my emotions from her.

"Yes, alright? Yes, they told me to walk away. They filled my head with lies. They told me it would be better for you and for me in the long run, to leave you before we were married. They said you wouldn't look at me the same. That you would consider me half a woman and one day would run out on me. You would cheat and leave me because I couldn't give you children. Is that what you want to hear? How my parents, the two people who never treated me as if I were their daughter because I hated how we lived, because I was the child who would much rather wear a pair of worn-out blue jeans and a ratted-up sweatshirt from a second-hand store instead of shopping on Rodeo Drive, or because I fell in love with a young man who lived in a foster home, deceived me? They tore my heart out right along with the parts of me that left me unable to become a mother, and I have hated them every day for it. What good is any of it going to do now, Tyson? None of it mattered when I could never give you something you wanted." Jesus fucking Christ. There it is. The ice-cold truth. I've known it all along. Felt it deep. And I'm raging to yank the knife out of my chest and smash it into the black hole of the ones responsible for taking her away from me. For watching her sit here and tell me it was for my protection. What a crock of smelly bullshit.

"It matters to me. To me, Lynne. I am not your father. I would have never done what he did or still does. All I wanted was you. I should have been your shield. Me. The one who would have walked that road with you. Protected you from all the darkness. The pain, the hurt. I would have never walked away." The urgent need to touch her has me moving forward to kneel down in front of her. I reach up and hold her tear-stained face in between my hands. I will never be able to take her pain away from her; she has to live with what she's done. However, I can be a bigger man than her father ever will be and tell her the words she desperately wants to hear.

"I'm so sorry it has taken me this long to tell you, Tyson. You'll never know how many times over the years I tried to gather the courage to find you and tell you that. The guilt has haunted me for years. After all this time, the cuts are still deep. I've bled for so long. I just…I can't live with this anymore." Christ, her tortured expression punctures my soul. It tears me right down the middle. Scattering parts of me everywhere.

"This is a lot to process for both of us. Give me some time. While doing that, you need to start forgiving yourself. It took bravery for you to come here and pour your heart out. To dig up old wounds and face me. Do you know how proud I am of you for that?" Her gasping wails echo around my apartment. They bleed into my walls, seep into my skin, and stop my heart. I've committed years to hating this woman for leaving me the way she did. For shutting me out from something no woman should have to choose to do. How can I hate her when it's clearly written all over her that she hates herself?

"Oh, God. Please tell me you mean that? That you are not saying it to pacify me or to get me out of your life?" she stutters through her sobs.

"I'm a man of my word, Lynne. I don't say anything I don't mean," I vow.

"You were always that way. So honest and trustworthy. Thank you," she says as she extends her hands to wrap around mine. Her touch is excruciatingly familiar. I can't stop my body from leaning into hers no matter how hard I try. The need to kiss her is stronger than the eagerness I had moments ago to touch her.

"Don't cry anymore," I say, my lips slowly getting closer. Her bloodshot eyes dart down to my mouth. The edges of her lips lift ever so slightly. God, her mouth was always the part of her that undid me. So many wonderful things have been spoken out of it. "It's so hard not to want to kiss you right now." I hope those words I said to her the first time I kissed her surface to the forefront of her memory. There's no going back in time for Lynne and me. I'll regret touching her, kissing her, and allowing my hands to feel her skin. So many unspoken words are still left to be said, and yet I find a hint of peace trying to surface. In time, maybe it will.

"You won't be able to stop kissing me once you start." I close my eyes at hearing her say what she said to me all those years ago.

"Probably not," I repeat what I told her many full moons before.

My lips meet her cheek. Softly. Tentative at first. I'm dying here. A wish-fulfilled death to kiss her lips. I can't go there. Not yet. Her lips burn like fire down my skin when I pull back slightly and she returns a kiss to my hand. I want her to feel the agony in my heart from missing her, losing her, and wanting badly to get to know her again. She didn't put her trust in our love. I need time to adjust. To move past this and her lack of trust in what we had. The internal struggle of forgiveness.

I remember our first kiss as I stare into her shiny eyes. How it turned frantic, mouths pressing together, tongues entwined. She tasted as good as she felt. Sweet, loving and fuck, I couldn't stop devouring her mouth. The beautiful girl who wanted me as much as I wanted her.

"You should go." I release my hold on her face. I don't miss the disappointment she's trying to hide from me asking her to leave. "I'll be in touch. I promise." Those are the last words I say to her as I push myself up, watch her stand, and wipe the tears off her face.

"I'll be waiting," she says with a slight smile. I don't regret her stopping by at all. The only thing I do regret is not going to her all those years ago when I first found out the truth. I wanted to so many times. Possibly more than she wanted to tell me. I fought it out of fear, further rejection, and for all the years she broke me. I wanted to die when I found out she had married. I became angry and bitter toward my best friends. Didn't give two shits about anyone or anything after that. I became violent, out of control, and it turned into a habit I didn't want to ignore.

Lynne was the only one in the world who made me feel as if I was good enough to accomplish anything. My grades perked up because of her. My desire to enlist and become a cop became a reality because of her, but Lynne, she turned our dreams into nightmares.

The irony of this situation isn't lost on me that everywhere I went, every woman I fucked reminded me of her. It's a sick feeling that twists my gut as I stand here staring at my closed door. When she left me, she took the important part of me with her. My heart. And now I see things clearly. She's carried it with her all along.

We've never stopped loving each other.

CHAPTER FOUR

LYNNE

There used to be times I would wake up in a cold, damp sweat. My dreams were always disappearing as quickly as my therapist said they'd run through my head. Dreams are natural; everyone has them. I know this. I've studied hard to develop how dreams can or can't become a reality. It's one of the many tricks a human mind plays. It's up to us to remember the ones that have a meaning behind them.

I knew Tyson was in most of mine. Even the nightmares that woke me in that cold, damp sweat. He was there. Always. Then there were times, like now, when my dreams are peaceful, content, and the thought of waking up and getting out of bed is a routine task I wish I didn't have to endure. But instead to lie here and pretend he was still holding me, whispering in my ear to have a great day or how much he loved me. How the way life cheated me out of becoming a mother was okay because we had each other and the love we had would conquer any obstacle life tossed our way.

I knew going over to his place and finally revealing the dreadful truth to him was going to be hard. I expected him to slam the door in my face. To yell at me to leave him alone the same way he did both of the times I've seen him. A sense of relief mixed with fear rushed over me when he invited me into a place that was as vulnerably naked as we were. The man lives like a recluse. There was no sign of life except him in his apartment anywhere. It's barely a home. Empty.

When I walked past him, it felt similar to having a bucket of ice dumped on my head. His vibes chilled me right to my bones. Then, as time progressed and I let myself open up and tell him the words I have wanted to say for years, it was if we both started to thaw. The block of ice dripping as he began to shed the hindering frozen obstruction of hatred he had for me. I felt it. I know I did.

What he feels for my parents, though, that will never go away. I don't blame him at all. I've lived with it every day for years. If I thought he hated them before, then I'm a bigger fool than I already am. He drove a truck into the side of my parents' house out of anger a few months back. I may be a fool, but I'm not an idiot. He did it to retaliate against me. He thought it would hurt me if he got to them. It did the opposite. I laughed until I couldn't anymore. When I told Maggie about it, somehow more joy seeped out of me. It still does when I think about it. It's a damn shame my parents weren't standing in front of it.

Tyson also touched a part of me I knew was there. It always has been. He replaced it with something new, fresh, and I dare to dream a beginning I never expected. It happened the minute he knelt down and touched me. His eyes started rejuvenating my soul. Stirring parts of me back to life. He had comforted me before he opened his mouth and without any hesitation at all told me he needed time. He placed a bind over my wounds, replaced my backbone, and left me with a wishbone that maybe, possibly, we could start anew. I know its wishful thinking on my end with all the deceit and betrayal between us. I'm trying hard not to get my hopes up, but the way he kissed me tenderly on my cheek is so fresh on my mind that it's all I can think about. All I've hope for. And I'm so scared and alone right now that I'm more frightened than the day I wrote that damn letter of good-bye.

I sigh, push back the covers, and run my fingers across the horizontal scar across my lower abdomen. The jagged, ugly reminder of the truth. The actuality that there is only one thing in life that is guaranteed, and that is death. I truly think I died that day. My heart, soul, and spirit were ripped out before I had a chance to live. All of it stripped away with the one word no one ever wants to hear. Cancer.

It struck me hard. Burned me out and happened just a few weeks before I was able to become his wife and escape the cruelty of my parents. To be happy and live a life with him.

My parents aren't responsible for what happened to my body. They didn't wish for me to be sick. For me to go through months of chemo, radiation, and to fall so deep into a black hole that it took years to see a sliver of light. No, they took their young daughter who couldn't think straight because her life was flying before her eyes and convinced her that she would be better off in the long run if she left the boy she loved.

So, like the rest of the world, I say, fuck cancer. I'm a survivor. A statistic. And I deserve to live. Deserve to be a happy. And somehow, I'm going to find it.

"Shit." I sit up abruptly when my phone starts vibrating, swing my legs over, and watch the screen light up with my sister Larissa's name. Why do people seem to always call at the wrong time? Especially her. I don't know if I want to answer it. I sigh again while it continues to ring. I said I would cut all of them out of my life. Do I do it now or simply ignore her?

I reach for the phone and hope it's not a mistake. "Good morning," I answer, my voice sounding chipper when I'm anything but. If she's calling in regards to my conversation with our mother about doing a ribbon-cutting ceremony, I'm hanging up on her.

"Woah. Someone sounds happy this morning." I roll my eyes, stumble to the kitchen, and push the button on my coffee pot, refusing to give her any bit of information. The less she knows, the better off I will be.

"It's a new day," I repeat what I always say when I talk to her. Larissa may love the lifestyle she leads, but she has always been the peacemaker in the family. She simply wants everyone to get along; out of everyone in my family, she's the only one I've confided my true feelings to. It hasn't changed her mind or made her take off her ugly shade of blinders. None of them understand that power means weakness to me, and thanks to being under my parents' thumb, she's too afraid to speak her mind. So, in other words, her call doesn't surprise me in the least. I'm going to miss her. One can only hope she won't cut Elizabeth out of my life. That little girl is the only one in this family who matters to me.

"It is, and I'm happy for you. Are your books filled with new clients?" She asks with enthusiasm. *Is our mother standing right next to you?*

"I wish. I do have a couple appointments today," I muster out with as much eagerness as I can. I'm nervous and excited. These are the first sessions I've had. It took years to get through school, to sit through required supervised practice with patients only to turn around and have to apply, go through a series of questions, and then take the state of California licensed test, and now here I am ready to take on this career that helped get me through the darkest part of my life.

"That's wonderful, Lynne. I'm proud of you. We all are." *Right*, I think to myself. Our parents couldn't care less. Laney has her head so far up our parents' ass that she wouldn't care if they took turns shitting her and her husband Sebastian out. That leaves Larissa and Jamie, her husband. If I were a betting woman, the odds would be against Jamie. Larissa could swing either way if she wanted. Power is money. Money is power to every single one of them. So, no. I highly doubt them being proud of me is high up on anyone's priority list.

"I know," I lie, soothing an argument with her which would lead to her telling me to get over it and that we are all family and should simply get along. I think that ship has sailed and sunk a long time ago.

"Listen, I have to make this quick. I wanted to tell you that Mom and Dad are on a rampage over you and whatever you have going on down there with Tyson. I tried talking to both of them last night. They won't listen. I wanted you to know that I stand behind you one hundred percent, Lynne. Out of any of us, you deserve to be happy, and I'll do whatever I can to make sure they don't interfere this time." I blink back tears at the memory of waking up in the hospital, my womanly parts gone. My body feeling foreign and my heart unforgiving to everyone around me. All I wanted was to have Tyson there when I woke up. Instead, I became alert and stared into the smirking, bright, explosive eyes of my father. He was secretively telling me he had won. That Tyson was gone and was never going to find me. I cried for hours, became hysterical and screamed for the man I loved. I was eighteen years old. Could make decisions for myself, and yet there I lay, lifeless and putty in my own parents' hands.

"You're calling to tell me you stood up for me and you want to support me? Come on, Larissa. We both know that's bullshit. You would much rather I be there, ending the chaos I've caused instead of here. That's why you're calling, isn't it? You want me to come there so we can talk, and when I do, you'll all attack me. Speak the truth, for God's sake," I snip, while her silence is all the proof I need that she's as full of as much deceitfulness as they are. She would be twelve kinds of stupid if I told her some of the things I know. "Say you are telling the truth. Then we both know your words won't do a damn thing. I'm not the same little girl I was back then. They've stripped me bare, Larissa. Deceived me in ways I will never understand. I can never have a child of my own, but one thing I do know is I would never make him or her a victim to my own personal agenda. They are both grasping a hold of the short end of a straw, because they know I'm not like them. I never have been. I never will be. After my talk with Mom yesterday, I told myself I was done with them, and now hearing this, I know for sure I am. So, you tell them to bring it on. I will destroy them, you, Laney, and anyone else. I will never allow anyone to try and hurt Tyson again. I love you, but I have to go." I hang up on her the same way I did my mother. It's rude. I know it. I simply choose not to care.

Larissa has no idea how evil my parents can be. How persevering they are. She's blinded like everyone else in their circle. If she fights my battles for me, she will be kicked out of that circle. That's on her, not me. I'm sick and tired of fighting with all of them.

I pour myself a cup of coffee, shut off my phone after I read a text from Larissa telling me how sorry she is and she loves me, and stride out to my deck. The morning sun shines down on my face; the smell of the ocean is calling my name. It's heaven here.

I sigh, wipe a tear from my face, and let my mind wander to my entire family. My heart is aching over the fact that I'm all alone. A family bond shouldn't be like this. It should be supportive, full of laughter, happiness, and hand holding. It shouldn't be about one sister sneaking around to tell the other to watch her back because of the power and influence their parents have. My sisters should have had my back long ago when this all started. They knew it destroyed me. Saw it in my eyes when they came to visit and I refused to talk, saw it every time I did or did not come home.

"I want nothing to do with any of you," I muse, sip my coffee, and jump when I see Vivian and Cora standing directly in front of me. Great. What else is going to rain down on my head today?

"We don't blame you at all for not wanting anything to do with us. We've treated you poorly. We came to apologize," Vivian says with a steady voice. My jaw smacks and falls between the cracks on my deck.

"Those words weren't meant for you. Sorry. Odd timing." I stumble around my own thoughts, composing myself in the process. Fairly positive these two women are here because Jude told them to come ease my mind. Why? None of them have a thing to gain except to bid me farewell.

"Are you alright? We didn't mean to intrude," Cora asks, her eyes whirring with sincerity. My troubled mind is telling me not everyone has a personal vendetta to hurt me, so stop jumping to conclusions. Be nice.

"You're not intruding. As far as being alright, I'm getting there." I shrug casually. My guard is up over these women. I've been that way around females most of my life. Growing up with my last name in one of the most powerful cities in the world, you either fit in with the crowd of the privileged or you don't. I never did, nor did I want to. I slept under the same roof as fake people. The desire not to be around them all day when I was at school churned my gut. I stayed as far away from them as I could. That's what led me to meet Tyson. The underprivileged tend to be kinder, hold loyalty with speaking the truth, and are appreciative of any- and everything life has to offer. They work hard and take nothing for granted.

"Well, then, for what it's worth, we truly are sorry for the way we've treated you. We saw you out here and decided it was time to tell you."

"Thank you, Vivian, I appreciate that," I tell her honestly, then turn my attention back to Cora.

"Your wedding was beautiful. Congratulations," I faintly mumble while blinking back the memories of all the tears that fell that night. It's difficult for me to speak about a wedding out loud. How I got through marrying Robert, I'll never know. I'm pretty sure it was due to the fact I allowed my mother to pull the wool over my eyes once again. Gave her full reign because a part of me didn't care. Numb. Always so numb.

The queen of hell wouldn't have had it any other way to begin with. Even though she protested until the veins in her forehead popped out over me giving them no choice about marrying Tyson, she still demanded to take over, claiming no Chapman lady would be walking down the aisle in anything but style. I knew she was covering up her lies then just like she's hiding behind them now. *If she only knew that I know everything.*

Enough about her. These women are standing before me out of kindness. Brave and courageous just like their men.

Cora reminds me somewhat of myself. I've heard pieces about her and Riddick here and there. Not many people are as lucky as she is, and she doesn't strike me as the kind of woman who would take advantage of anyone, so acknowledging her wedding is the least I can do. Especially with the two of them showing how strong they are by coming over here.

"Thank you. We'll let you get back to your coffee. We really are sorry for treating you poorly. Our only excuse, and it's the truth, is, we're a family. We care about one another, and well, you showing up out of the blue—"

"It's okay," I admit, stopping her before she says something that will spoil the god mood they have put me in. "I completely understand. You have no idea how much happiness it brought me to see Tyson has all of you." I know they aren't here to fish for information. I'm not in the frame of mind to talk about family, especially when my own flesh and blood hasn't a clue what the word means.

"Alright, then, have a good day. And we wish you luck with your new practice. The hospital is very lucky to have you." I grip my mug tightly, suddenly feeling self-conscious and nervous around the two of these highly-educated women.

"Thank you," I reply awkwardly. It seems they know more about me than I do them. Which isn't surprising with as tight as they all are. I've also seen the two of them at the hospital a few times when I went to introduce myself to administration. The entire staff welcomed me with open arms. Took several of my business cards and showed me around.

The two patients I have today were referrals from the hospital.

I watch them walk in the opposite direction of our homes. Jealousy pings at my gut over how close they are. I'm not sure where our relationship will go from here, but a warm feeling sinks into my heart, the same feeling I had about a new beginning when I talked with Tyson. I stand there holding my now cold coffee cup in my hands. My eyes start drifting to the ocean, and for the first time in as long as I can remember, I allow another genuine smile to graze my lips. I won't push them to become my friends, to welcome me into their tiny bubble. However, I do feel a weight of relief lifted off my shoulders knowing that a tiny hole has been punctured allowing us to all breathe in the same air.

***

"How did it go?" Maggie asks after the last of my two patients schedules her next appointment and slips out the door. I feel horrible for the young lady who I've just spent the past two hours with. Our first appointment should have been a get-to-know-you type of thing. Instead, she jumped right in the minute I asked her why she felt the need to see me. I should have assessed her situation. Saved that second hour for our next session. In its place, I held her hand while the poor thing cried her heart out over being the sole survivor of an automobile accident that wasn't her fault. It killed her two best friends. I couldn't ask her to leave, and now as I hand Maggie her file, I second-guess myself. This job is going to test every fiber in my body. I'm going to treat people whose paths in life are similar to mine. It scares me to death.

"It went well," I respond, not wanting to make her worry. She freaked out the other day after Jude left here. Maggie is a worrywart when it comes to me, and I couldn't love her more for it. "What are these?" I change the subject when I notice a big bouquet of forget-me-nots, white roses, daisies, and lilies sitting on her desk.

"They're for you." She reaches over and plucks out the attached card and hands it to me. The writing on the envelope whispers across my skin and touches my naked soul.

"Are they from him?" she probes, her voice breaking. The first thing I did when I returned home was call and tell her all about my visit with

Tyson. Then this morning, I went into telling her about my call from my sister and my admission to myself that I'm better off severing ties with all of them. None of them are going to change the way they feel, and for Larissa to be caught in the middle will eventually make her resent me even if she puts herself there. When I told her about the quick chat I had with Cora and Vivian, she broke down in tears of happiness.

"Yes," I answer as I slip my finger under the seal to open it.

"What does it say?" She stands, peering over my shoulder to read it.

The writing is scratchy, barely legible, but it's his. I would recognize it in my sleep. Tyson has always had the worst handwriting.

Lynne,

Good luck today. I know you'll do great. I'd like to take you to dinner tomorrow night. Be ready by 6:30. I'll pick you up at your house. Tyson

I've never smiled so wide in my entire life.

CHAPTER FIVE

TYSON

I wake with another hard-on. Bigger than the one I woke with yesterday. No morning wood here. It's all her. The woman of every fantasy I've had.

When Lynne left the other night, I locked up, went straight to bed, and tossed and turned with long lost memories floating through my head. My reality blurred the lines of the animosity I've felt for her. I began to defrost, and it scared the fuck right out of me. My nerves ate away at my stomach. Branding me into a curled-up fetal position of balled-up torment. I hated it and loved it at the same damn time.

I knew who Lynne was before we met. The odd, beautiful rich girl. The one who didn't quite fit in anywhere. I felt the same way she did. I grew up as a state welfare child. Living with a family who acquired me for money. They didn't give a shit about me or anyone else. They provided me with a home, food, and clothes. Nothing more. Nothing less.

It took days for me to gather the courage to talk to Lynne, to ask her why she was wandering down the hall where we poor kids hung out. One day, I gathered that courage, sat by her at lunch, and we easily started talking about the book of poetry she was reading. I couldn't have cared less about it, but it intrigued her, so I listened. When the five-minute alert bell rang, I walked her to class, left her there, and stayed clear until the next day, when I sat next to her again. Our conversations turned into talking about everything from the weather to the clothes some of the kids wore to school. I asked her out, we became inseparable, and she fought daily with her parents about me. I never knew what the word love meant until I fell for that innocent green-eyed girl. Love is the highest emotion of them all. You can fly, or you can crash. You can feel, or you can go numb. It's a tricky thing to live with, and I've denied it for a long time.

I hated that I came between her and her family. Especially when I never had a real one myself, but when she convinced me she was nothing like them, I stayed away, let her handle them until the day I was ready to enlist. I couldn't go without her. So, I bought a ring with a diamond you could barely see, asked her to marry me, and we started to plan; that is, until her mother stepped in calling me names whenever I called, and her father asked to see me. *I wonder if she still has the ring.*

I never told her any of this. On how he tried to tear me a new asshole. Tried to buy me off. I had hated that measly fucker before he tried handing me fifty thousand dollars to walk away. There was something in his beady little eyes that told me he was being forced to give me that money. I cast it aside as quickly as I did the money. The man was and still is too much of an arrogant prick to let anyone tell him what to do. Every day since then, I've wanted to kill the son of a bitch for not putting his daughter's happiness before his own. I told him to fuck off and if he didn't give her the wedding she wanted, I would expose him to the world. He blanched, his head shot back, and I explained about seeing him leaving the house down from mine several times during the day and night. That was the first time I found out he was fucking around behind his wife's back. He caved just as easily as he defied my relationship with his daughter. He's a pussy, a coward, and he's the grit behind taking Lynne's sickness and twisting it to his own fucked-up pleasure. I'm going to demolish him and anyone who stands in my way for what they've done.

Lynne's words of what good will any of it do echo in my head. It will do me good to know I've destroyed him, and if he makes one move to try and drive a wedge between us, he's as good as dead. I'll ruin him and his precious reputation. I'll fuck that entire family up the ass with information, and I'll be damn sure to stand there and watch their empire crumble.

I roll my body out of bed, my dick soft and throbbing. The minute I crank on the shower, I look in the mirror and tell my reflection I'm changing. The old Tyson is back, and he's going to fight for what he wants. I have to, or I'll become a dead man over this. I'm not ready to forgive her just yet, but I'm willing to try. To talk and will the strength I possess to help both of us heal.

I have plans for Lynne today. No more thinking of that lousy fucking excuse of a father of hers, not until after I put her first.

My hand slides down the length of my cock the minute I step in and allow the heated water to soak into my skin. The more he grows, the more painful he becomes. God, I ache for her. This is wrong in so many ways. My dick should not be coated by my hand; it should be coated by her pussy, her mouth, her hand, and yet here I am taking a shower before work thinking of Lynne. Stroking my dick with a reminder of the way she was looking at my naked chest. She wanted to touch me as badly as I did her. Christ, how I wish she were here with her legs spread wide and my face in between them.

With one excruciating painful talk, the woman has made her way back into my life, and it sheds a dead layer of skin from me, leaving clean flesh that could easily be diced into pieces. I should be running, avoiding her at all costs. I can't. Now that she's admitted the truth, it's dulled the burn. Aspired my fantasies. And I'm riding some sort of high that she found the strength to find me herself. To explain in her words and not someone else's that she was wrong.

I stroke my cock with one hand while rolling my balls in the other, my fingers gliding over the slicked head. The veins are angered and protrude out. Closing my eyes, I try and remember the last time Lynne and I were together. Teenagers, exploring, learning, and driving one another mad with burning desire. I loved her more than I could begin to describe. I cherished her, wanted to give her everything when I had nothing to give except a young man with goals to make the woman he loved happy. It was enough for her. I was enough. I know I was.

Everything we did together put a smile on her face; the movies, roller skating, or simply swimming at the beach. My girl didn't need the fancy shit. The high-class parties where the parents sat around discussing who made more money that day, while the kids secretively snuck out to drink a bottle of expensive whiskey they stole from their parents' stock. She wanted me. A poor white boy.

My dick swells in my hands from remembering the first night we made love. I worked her body with my mouth, my fingers, and eventually we explored sex for the first time, together. I never took her roughly, always slowly, passionately, and it was the best fucking feeling in the world to make love to her. Right now, as the first squirt of my come hits the wall of my shower, I'd give anything to experience that all over again, to make love instead of fuck. Or to fuck while making love to her. A face that has never escaped my mind. A woman who has never left my heart and who never will.

***

"What the fuck do you think you're doing? Get your boots off my desk, asshole." I shove Riddick's legs off the edge of my desk after dropping a couple of files off to my captain. Both his and Jude's laughter rings out in the small area of the precinct the three of us share. *Jerks.*

"Fuck off. Neither one of us has spoken to you since the other day. You were pissy and shitting down everyone's throats for two weeks. The normal Tyson, and now today, you've been sitting there with a smile all over your face. Something's going on. So, the way I see it, I can't have my new boots covered in the horseshit that's piling up in here, man. Either you finally talked it out with Lynne, and Christ, I hope that's it, or you hit your head on the sidewalk." I feel the skin around my eyes crinkle upward. I do owe them some sort of explanation for my behavior today. Shit, I owe them justification for years of being a complete and utter bastard.

These two were out in the field yesterday, while I worked the desk. I called in for flowers to be delivered, did my job, and went straight home. This morning, I came in and set about doing some paperwork while making a call to Dane to run a check on Lynne's father for me. Dane has a nose like a K9, ears like a bat, and eyes as sharp as a nocturnal animal's in the night. He can sniff out when a person took their last piss, and I'm going to have him dig until he can find something other than Richard's marital discretions to wrench that prick down from his throne. I know the dirty Hollywood leech is sucking the blood out of someone. Covering his tracks. Whatever it is, I'm going to find out.

Now, I'm sitting here trying to figure out where to take her tonight. She and I still need to talk, sort things out, and we can't do it publicly. That leaves two options, her place or mine. And there is no way in hell she's coming back to my place, not until I can treat her the way a woman should be treated. Fuck, I don't even own a set of pots and pans, let alone a table for her to eat at.

"I talked with Lynne the other night. There are things I need to tell you, just not here." Jude meets my eyes, grinning like a damn fool, while Riddick's brows rise a notch, his eyes not blinking for several drawn-out seconds. I squeeze my eyes shut when his expression begins to soften. I've been at the opposite end of many stare downs from him. Over half of them, I was too drunk to remember. When I open them to witness a gleam of thankfulness in his eye instead of disappointment, anger, or frustration, it eases more of the dull ache in my chest. It's a short-lived look. One he's experienced along the same stretch of highway. It's having your heart beat rapidly in your throat when you think of the woman you've always loved. When you see her face, hear her voice, and push your anger over the edge of a cliff, allowing it to die and to replace your life with gratitude, happiness, and the knowledge of starting over or finishing where you left off.

"Tyson, we've waited years for you to fill us in. We'll wait as long as it takes. This isn't about us; it's about you and her." I have to look away after hearing Jude say that. For years, I've lived a life full of hate, trying to put my mind into a coma by fucking, drinking, and doing things I'm ashamed to admit. It was the only way I could erase her from my head. To take away the anger, the pain that held my heart captive in unbreakable chains. Not once did I turn to my two best friends, who are before me now telling me to get on with it. To do what I feel is right for me. I feel the weight being lifted already.

"I'm ready. Let me get through tonight with her." I shoot them a sly grin. They've worried about me enough. I'm done hurting them. Done hurting myself over something that was completely out of my control.

"We're here whenever you're ready," Riddick replies with a cocky smirk.

"I appreciate it. You mind telling me what that grin is for?" His smile widens; it's damn close to blinding me.

"Richard Chapman. Are you going after the dirtbag? Because if you are, that's one Goddamn situation you aren't shutting us out of. I want that motherfucker about as badly as you do." I doubt that. Although with the shit he did to Cora, I'll allow him to stand second in line.

"You bet your ass I am. It would be my pleasure to slap some cuffs on him, watch him squirm, and interrogate him all the way to prison," I answer furiously.

"I'm already on it. There's no way he hasn't done anything wrong. He's too shady to be clean," Jude snaps. Fingers are clicking away on the keys of his laptop. Fuck me. I don't deserve these two, but fuck all if my insides aren't lighting up like a stormy sky. I fucking love these guys.

"You know I can handle him, right? I mean, come on, don't you two think you've been through enough?"

"Not when it comes to family, we haven't," Jude implies, lifts his chin my way without looking up from his screen. My heart has been bleeding out for years, holes poked until there have been days I didn't want to live, and here I stand with tears in my eyes over this selected family of mine I couldn't have hand-picked any better if I had tried.

"I feel the same way. You good if I take off?" I bid, pushing my emotions down.

Jude peaks over the edge of his glasses, a choked-out laugh escaping his throat. "Man, you're scaring the piss out of me with being all nice and shit. Before you go, I want you to know I went and spoke with Lynne the other day."

I knew that motherfucker had something up his sleeve after talking to him in the hall. "She told me," I lie. I'm not going to chew his ass out for having my back. What I will do is acknowledge him for having it. I'll let Lynne know Jude told me and leave it at that. If his talk pushed her to come see me, then so be it. It's done, over, and I'm moving on. "I'll catch you both later."

Emotions controlled, I grab my helmet off my desk, make my way down the hall and out the door with not a care in the world except for treating Lynne right. It's an unaccustomed feeling that grips me by the balls and squeezes my lungs. The only thing that matters to me at this moment is thoroughly talking this out. As I crank up my bike and start to weave my way toward her house, a thought of how to do that strikes me. It's been so long since I've dated. Hell, I'm hoping my sensors are remotely correct and she's on the same page as I am. I need her back even if everything we say to each other lashes out and strikes my skin hard.

Everything looks foreign to me as I pull down her small street, one I've been down many times. It's as if I'm reliving a part of my life all over again. The part where a young kid shows up in a neighborhood he shouldn't be in. All those memories fade when I come to a stop in her driveway, flip up the shield on my helmet, and watch her climb out of her car with a grocery bag in her hands. Her eyes locking shocked onto mine.

I've wished many times to be able to resemble an intense moment like this. Where I could set the pause button on my life, press rewind, or fast forward to monumental instances similar to this. For my wife to be waiting for me to come home. Dinner. Laughter and this spark. God, this flaming spark between her and me. To be able to experience some of the best feelings in my life over and over again. They would never grow old. They would never stop, and I would never get tired of seeing her look at me this way. I feel her energy from here. It's pulling me toward her, tugging at the tattered strings on my heart. Sucking me into the world I'm welcoming with open arms.

Questions flurry across her face. Answers dangle in the warm breeze of the air. It's time to battle. Time to win the war that's been beating me down for thirteen years. I can do this. I can be the man I was meant to be. For her.

Her contact roams over my face as I tug off my helmet. It's full of a powerful passion that sets my soul on fire.

"Hi," she says. The sound of her sweet voice is enough for me to realize that this is really happening. That the opportunity to put my life back together is standing mere feet away from me in a white off-the-shoulder top, a pair of black shorts, and heels with a strap winding around her ankle and ending shy of her knees. I'm fucked. Royally screwed. She's stunning.

"Hey." I hang my helmet on the handlebars, swing my leg around, and make my way to her. I would hang the moon right now to be able to pick her up and carry her inside the house. To strip her of everything but those heels and take my time memorizing every dip, every curve, and every shape of her body. It's a slow-burning ache that has subdued my conscious mind. It's draining my brain. Running a ruckus of years of pent-up emotional hazards that I've spent hating her right out of my open veins and melting them into the hot cement below my feet.

"I…um…I thought we could have dinner here. Maybe sit on the beach and talk." A breath expels out of those pink-stained plump lips. Lips I need to taste and memorize again.

"Either that or you can hop on the back of my bike." *Preferably with those shoes on.* I'm not hungry for food. I'm hungry for her. I need to cram it down about a thousand knots, or I'll be fucking her and regretting it. Our relationship is delicate. Hell, I don't even know what to call it at this point. A new beginning. Fuck if I know what's happening here. I'm all in down this free-flowing highway once we get over the speedbumps, the potholes, and the curves that have slowed us down. Until then, my cloudy thoughts need to stay lodged in my dirty little intellect.

"Um. If that's what you want." She bites her bottom lip. My dick screams, *I'm down here.*

"Another time. Tonight, I'd like to sit around and talk." She releases her lip, smiles, and sighs. I'm totally screwed.

"Thank you for the flowers. Would you mind?" She hands me the bag, bends down, and gives me the perfect view of her ass as she leans in her car and retrieves the giant vase out of a box. Fuck. My thoughts aren't going anywhere. My hands, however, want to grip her hips, shove her ass into my groin and allow her to wiggle. To let her see what she's doing to me. Fucking hell. My dick is really screaming now.

"You're welcome," I answer, swallowing. I'm a nervous wreck. A stranded man along the road in the dark. Fucked and screwed over. Hurt and bleeding out, and there is more to come.

"I love them, Tyson. You remembered my favorite color."

"I remember everything about you, Lynne." I close my eyes wishing I could inhale those words back. That ache hitting me square in the chest again. I hate that I'm hurting her. "Damn it. I didn't mean it in a bad way."

"I know, Tyson. It's going to take time. I have all the time in the world. Let's go inside," she says with sorrow. It's her eyes, though, that give me hope, which simmer with the one memory I can't ignore. Lynne is looking at me as if I'm the world she's talking about. I'm all the way in. Heart, head, body, and soul.

CHAPTER SIX

LYNNE

I'm not sure what I expected after shockingly reading the card from Tyson. It scared me to the point I broke down with fresh tears. I cried for more reasons than my mind could process at the time, and before this is all over, I'll cry more.

After all these years, he remembered my favorite color, and the flowers are absolutely beautiful. I began to wonder if he committed to his memory all of our talks and dreams the way I have. Did he think about me often? Birthdays, holidays. Did he ever fall in love again? Did he buy a home in the country where there was nothing but rolling hills and green for as far as the eyes could see?

Fancy restaurants, fast cars, and mansions on a hill are an important possession to the wealthy. The rich love to brag, to outdo one another. None of those things trump finding true love. None of them come remotely close to being in the same atmosphere, and here I am with the common knowledge all along that being loved and giving it freely in return is the most important possession I will ever own; and yet I've done nothing to bring my one true love back to me. *You're doing it now. You went to see him. That was a start.*

I allowed Maggie to hold me in the middle of my office, to tell me she had faith and the tears should be ones of happiness. No more broken hearts. Not when I can mend them.

Maggie immediately wiped my tears away, took hold of my face, and told me to leave. To go home. I left. Curled up in a ball and cried. For hours, I sank. Lower and lower I sunk into a turbulent funk. Tyson's voice drifting the further I slipped away.

I lay there staring out into the starry sky. Not moving until the sun started to rise this morning. Work was slow. Maggie sent me home again and shoved me out the door with my flowers in my hand.

By the time I pulled into my drive, took a shower, and made myself presentable, I no longer wanted to go out in public. I wanted Tyson for myself. To be able to talk to him without interruptions. To find out as much as I could about him. So, I left, went to the grocery store, and turned back time in my head. I bought all of the things I remembered he loved to eat. Tacos, burgers, hotdogs. America's favorite foods. I even bought a jar of cherries. Tyson would get so angry trying to tie a knot with a stem, while me, I could tie one in less than a minute. I have no idea how I learned to do it; it came naturally, I guess.

"They were finishing remodeling this place when Riddick bought his house. Always wondered how the inside looked," Tyson admits from behind me. He's not even touching me and yet my skin becomes alive with an awareness I've never felt before. God, I want him to touch me, to own me. To make me soar.

He's so close to me that his scent invades a hidden unfamiliarity that I could drift into unknown waters. It hurts my heart. He doesn't smell the same, sound the same, or even look the same. It saddens me that I've missed out on his life. I'll spend the rest of my life paying for the one mistake that pulled us both under. How I've managed all these years with barely breathing I will never know. All that matters is he's here now. With me. Alone.

I take a deep breath inhaling this new scent. Memorizing it in case things go south here. I have no idea what his intentions are. I can only go by the things he said and did. He's a man of his word, and I have to believe he wants to get to know me again. It's all I've ever wanted. I'm afraid my life will end for good if he doesn't.

"I believe the setup downstairs is entirely different from Riddick's and Vivian's." I find my voice through the confinement of the grainy quicksand in my throat.

I speak this, because you can see their kitchens from the beach, whereas mine is in the middle of the house with the living room in the back. I love it that way. It brings me peace watching the waves, the dogs, the kids play. *Kids. Boys. Two of them.* No, I won't allow my thoughts to go there. Not today.

My wobbly legs carry me the rest of the way to my home. With fingers that tremble, I stick the key in the lock, turn the doorknob, and allow us both inside.

"Jesus, Lynne. This is…damn, it's nice." I smile, set the vase of flowers on the white coffee table, and pull my shoulders back. I can do this. For me, for him.

"You're the first person besides my friend Maggie to see it." I gaze dreamily around the room I practically live in. The cream-colored furniture with lavender pillows, a deep, dark purple wall on one side with a massive stone fireplace and television resting above. The rest of the walls are a pale shade of cream with stained glass mirrors and matching candle sconces that when the sun shines, reflect a kaleidoscope of colors. It's airy, refreshing, and the two sets of French doors with small paned glass windows in between are what sold me on the place. It gives me a complete view of the beach and ocean.

"I heard you and Maggie became friends. She's a great lady, and this place…It's all you. What the hell is that?" His mood shifts when his eyes train on something across the room. I follow them and immediately catch onto what he sees. He sets the bag down on the hardwood floor, takes a few long strides to the couch, and picks up the old, tattered camouflaged army blanket he received from his recruiter. I stand there mute, an idiot wondering what he'll think. Can he feel it, that the power of the love we once shared has never left me? Tyson gave it to me. He said it could keep me warm while he was at basic training. It was one of the few things I took from my childhood home when I left there for good.

I have to lock my knees to keep me from falling when tear-filled eyes gaze up into mine. My breath hitches; it's caught in my throat. "I… I couldn't part with it. I took it out of the box I had it stored in the minute I left my husband." I close my eyes as guilt slithers up my body; it coils itself tight and wraps around every part of me, crushing, constricting the air out of my lungs like a deadly snake. Damn it. I didn't want our night to start out this way.

I don't open my eyes. I can't. Betrayal and disloyalty crawl across my flesh. They itch, they burn, and they sting so much that I can't help but let the tears slip from the corners of my eyes.

"Don't hide behind your eyes. Open them and face me." His words feel like an anchor. They weigh me down, and I can't. I simply can't do this. I lose it, this waging battle. The conflict is too much. I'm suffocating inside of my own body.

"I'm so sorry, Tyson. So darn sorry. I'm dying here. I don't know what to say. What to do or even to think. I've waited a lifetime to see you. To hear your voice, to touch hold, let you hold me, and for you to tell me everything is going to be alright. It's not alright. How can you even begin to try and forgive me when I can't find it in me to forgive myself?" The ice in my veins isn't melting anymore. It's stuck. Sludging. Unshifting. Unmoving. I need him in my life so bad I throb. I can't make it on my own no matter how hard I try.

It all shifts the moment I feel the blanket around my shoulders. Tyson's warmth around me in a sweet, embracing hug. If he only knew how many sleepless nights I would curl up in a tight little ball with the security and comfort of this blanket wrapped around me. The memories, promises I should have kept, that I would wish were true. I've cried myself to sleep wishing we were underneath it together. Many times.

Suddenly, a strong, solid arm winds around my waist, another circles just above the back of my knees, and I'm lifted with ease in his arms. Not a thing in my life has felt this good. This real. This true.

"It's going to be okay. I promise. I've forgiven you; you need to believe that, Lynne. I wouldn't be here if I didn't." I struggle through my cries to grip hold of him tight. To try and have faith in what he's saying. It's the hardest thing to do when you've hated yourself for as long as I have. Forgiveness doesn't come easy, yet here I sit, curled up in the arms of the man I didn't have the strength to face. I've pretended to live in a world not meant for me. Every touch inspired by my own hand was his. Every swipe across my lips was his. Everything was his.

It belonged to only him.

"I left you standing at the end of a church aisle. How can anyone forgive someone for that? I don't deserve to be in your presence, Tyson." Fear lurks in the air. My cells lock up. It freezes me solid when he doesn't speak for the longest time. When I open my eyes, his expression is blank, focusing on his deep, deep thoughts. I wish I could read his mind, hear his opinions, or twist my mind to deem the acceptance that doubt and that awful feeling of dread don't belong here. Life is giving me a chance to live again. I've lived in the shadows of my fear for so long that it's a part of me. They've never disappeared.

"You need to listen to me. I'm going to say all of this one time, Lynne. Once. If you don't let it sink in and take my word for what it's worth, then whatever the future is supposed to hold for us may as well stop right here. I want words, baby. Words out of your pretty little mouth that you understand what I'm about to say. That you get me, because I've not once forgotten how much you mean to me. Not one damn day went by in all these years that I stopped caring about you." Oh, God. My heart thuds. My eyes snap open wider to his command.

Every word he said has sunk into my bones, from how much I still mean to him, how he hasn't forgotten, and his infatuation with my mouth. Tyson loved to talk. He loved to hear me speak. Express my thoughts, my feelings, and desires.

"There she is. The strongest woman I know. Give me the words I want to hear," he demands. I don't deserve the way he's beholding me in his gaze. Loving. Tender. Wanted.

"I hear you, Tyson," I choke through a heart-wrenching sob that squirms up from my gut. It ripples throughout me, and it hurts. His words are meant to settle me, but instead, they're the deserving open hand that slaps across my face. They burn, sting, and cause a sick sensation to curl in my stomach. I should have found the nerve to do this so long ago. I simply wasn't ready.

"Don't cry. Please. I hated it when you cried. I still do. Do you have any idea how strong of a woman you are? You didn't allow what happened to destroy you. You might think you did, but look at what you've done. You became a doctor. You took what life threw at you and in return, you are sacrificing to help others. I respect and admire you for that. You have more courage than anyone I have met. We have to face what happened together. In order for us to see past the pain, the hurt, you have to forgive, Lynne. As much as I want to help you, I can't. The one thing I can do is promise you I want to put it all behind us. To start over. Every part of me craves to get to know you again. I know you got married and it's a dick move on my part to say this right now, but fuck it. I hated him. Thought I hated you, too. It was never hatred I felt. It was jealousy, because in my heart, in my soul, and down to the depths of my despair, you belonged to me. Don't do this to you, to us. Don't give in to the guilt and shame anymore. I've dreamed long enough to hold you, to fall hard again with you. Let me take us there. Fall with me, Lynne."

Oh, sweet God.

I'm not sure when I stopped crying or breathing. His words are a metrical tune to my core. His mouth has spoken things I've dreamt about. His lips produced lyrics I've imagined to hear more times than I can count. Play. Pause. Repeat. He doesn't have to ask me to fall with him. I fell years ago. I never allowed him to catch me. Never gave him a chance. I'm afraid to tell him. Scared it will scare him away. He admits he cares, but love? He can't still love me the way I love him. It's entirely impossible, or is it? I don't know. I stare into his glossy eyes. Tyson is holding back years of tears. I can feel his heartbeat strumming, his body quivering, his chest rising and falling underneath the palm of my hand. He's showing his courage to fight those tears for fear I will break down again.

"This, you, those words. They mean everything to me, Tyson. It's not easy being on the other end of forgiveness. I'm still afraid of so many things." Slowly, I inch my hand over to place it directly across his beating heart. Warmth streams below my palm. My fingers are trembling from the inside out. They twitch to feel his skin. Momentum surges and my sobs are all forgotten. My pulse quickens when he grips my hand, tangles our fingers, and lays them back across the very same spot. I believe he has the same things running through his mind that I do. The need for the simplest touch.

"Tell me your fears, and I'll tell you mine. Let's start there, okay?"

he prods in a way that makes my stomach want to fly.

"I'm scared of everything. So many things that it fries my brain. You, me, life. Dying. I'm a cancer-free survivor, and I'm thankful for being able to breathe. But, Tyson, I may never know what it's like for someone to look up to me and call me mom. To be able to teach my child the important things in life. To hear them talk, walk, or watch them grow. I guess what I fear most of all is not being loved. Not being able to love someone so wholeheartedly that there isn't a thing you wouldn't do for them." He lifts his hand; the sweep of his fingers across my lips is a heated eruption to my heart. Gentle. Tender.

"Life isn't fair, is it? I've been unstable for years. Living a long list of black lies. Wishing there was some way, someone who would walk into my life and wake me up. Tell me I'm stumbling near death for some of the things I have done. Every day before today is our past, Lynne. It can't be undone, unchanged, or forgotten. You stormed back unexpectedly and did so without giving up. In the same way, like you, I'm scared to death to be alone. We aren't anymore. We can fight your demons together. You're a smart woman; you know there are other options out there to become a mom. Many of them. You just have to want it. Take it and live. Crawl out from the rock you've been hiding under and look at the gifts you do have. Stop blaming and start doing. I'm not going anywhere. Not until the last breath expels from my lungs. However, I won't deny I'm still struggling with you not trusting me or us enough for me to stand by your side. I'm still mourning the loss of our possible children. That's not something I can easily forget. But I'm willing to fight our fears together if you are." This is one of those moments where I want to pinch myself in order to be sure I'm not dreaming. I'm not, though, am I?

Suddenly, all I see is Tyson, a life lost, love, and a cherished moment where so many painful words were said. Regardless of how much hurt I've caused, the meaning behind them has shocked my heart back into action. It's cleansed my veins, opened my soul, and hit my system with a resounding need to confess everything. I want to tell him my hidden secret badly. Except I'm raw. Worn out. And I need for him and me to be a little more stable before I dump too much on him. So, I press my foot on the throttle and with everything I have in me, I continue on.

"Don't you see that I'm the one who made you feel that way? It was me. If I had never left you the way I did, you wouldn't have walked through life alone. You wouldn't be mourning children that I can never have," I choke out. I hate that he's feeling this way. The man I once knew would have made such a wonderful father. I honestly believe he still would. His heart is incredibly full.

"Not anymore, I don't. Not when I have you in my arms where you belong. We are being given something rare. A chance to start over. That is what I see. I see you. Open those eyes and look around. I'll say this again. Do you know how many times I would fall asleep at night wishing for this? To be close to you, to hold you, tell you I've loved you. We don't walk in another person's shoes. Or dream the same dreams unless two people were destined to be one. We are those two people; our steps can be the same; we can slip on our shoes and run if we want to. Don't look back at the heartache. Create something new, anything, just do it with me." My fear may be slipping away with each tiny breath I take; then again, there's more. One more emotion that continues to rip me apart. Always coiling me tight, always stepping over that fear to lead the pack off the line. I'm so rolled up right now in this one sensation I don't know what to think. Guilt.

"I had the same dreams. When I found out I had cancer and lost you, I died inside, Tyson. There were days I wished I really would have. It took me two years of therapy, wandering around the streets, sitting on park benches at night to watch the stars, hoping you would see them, too. Always wondering why I allowed my family to persuade me to hurt you the way I did. I knew it was wrong, yet I still went through with it. That right there is what's stopped me from moving forward on adoption, on moving my life past a young woman in love with a man who would have hung the moon and those stars for her. Guilt is an ugly, ugly thing. It's a part of me that blends and stirs my life into chaos every single day. The frustration builds inside of me until I feel like I'm going to explode. I hate being weak and broken." He wants me to flip a switch to the happy side of life when I'm unable to act as if what I did didn't break us both. Didn't make him feel the way he did. It's a constant habitual tear at my heart. But I feel my walls starting to crumble. My strength is coming back to allow me to begin healing.

"Guilt shouldn't play a role between you and me. The guilt should be on your parents. Tell me something, were they there for you?" My parents? If he only knew how I loathe them with all that is within me.

"No. Not in the way they should have been," I say, my tone growing angry. Whenever I mull over the shit I went through alone, my hate for my family grows like the ugly weeds you yank out of the ground, roots and all, yet somehow, they magically keep returning. They are despicable people.

"Then why feel guilt? Why not anger?"

"Oh, I feel anger every day. I have battle scars all over the place. My war I fought alone with guilt, shame, and hate. I never thought I could hate someone as much as I do them."

"You know I wouldn't have left you, Lynne. I'm not that guy. I'll repeat it every day for the rest of my life if I have to. I would have encouraged, not discouraged you. I would have been the strength you needed to find your own. And I would have never cheated on you because you couldn't give me a child. Not in this lifetime or the next. Not fucking ever." I reach up and rub the frown between his eyes. For one brief moment, I hold my finger there. Skidding it across the crease that begins to trouble his mind.

I feel his eyes on me. Deeply intense. Real. I'm in his arms.

"I know." I can't deny it. I've always known.

I can feel the fear in my chest wanting to emerge. I won't allow it to come skidding its way to a screeching halt in this room. Life has broken me down. I'm working my way back up to being happy. There's no room for any negative emotions here. I need to be positive.

Talking this out with him is quite possibly the hardest thing I've done. It's worse than waking up on the bathroom floor covered in my own vomit. Worse than what I learned about my father. It's challenging me in the most grueling way, and yet here I am fighting harder than anything I've fought for before. The one person I've always wanted. Him.

CHAPTER SEVEN

TYSON

"Is this for real? What kind of sick motherfucker would do this?" For the life of me, I can't swallow down what I'm reading. My stomach is contracting violently. I'm afraid I wouldn't make it to the bathroom if the acidic bile decided it wanted to come up and blend itself in with the hostile taste these papers are leaving in my mouth. This has got to be the lowest thing a man can do. Good God Almighty.

I'm sitting here at The Seasonal Lounge with Dane, Riddick, and Jude, going over Jude's recent discovery for us to pin Lynne's dad's ass to the fucking wall. Never in a million years did I expect to see information as horrendously ugly as this.

It's been two days since I've talked to Lynne. We've managed to work through some of the most gut-wrenching moments of our lives. Talked for hours, drank a few beers on her deck, ate food that I haven't eaten in years, and talked some more. I walked away after telling her our next form of communication was up to her. That both of us required time to allow everything we spoke to sink in.

This bit of information would bottle her progress right back up. It would mutilate the growth we've made. Possibly destroy us both if she were to find this out. *I won't keep it from her.*

"Secrets and lies are what tore us apart. I have to tell her." I look up at my friends, the file in my hand setting a new kind of fire to my skin. I'm ready to kill someone. My target: her father.

"It's true, man. Everything in that file is a copy from what I discovered in his office. That man is one sly son of a bitch," Dane adds, his jaw ticking, hands clenching into a fisted ball. If I didn't hate Richard as much as I do, I might feel sorry for the cock-sucking maggot if I were to give these guys the all clear to beat his ass.

"I trust you. It blows my fucking mind that he would do this. I need to tell you guys something. Once I do, I think you'll get a better understanding as to why I want to bury this guy." The weight of the folder feels heavy in my hands as I close it and drag my gaze to the dark green binder that could potentially hurt more people than Lynne.

Leaning forward, I drop it on the table, pick up my cigar, my bottle of beer, and take a long pull of both to calm my nerves. I need to concentrate on one thing at a time. Right now, I'm about to tell my brothers a story I should have told them a long time ago.

The room suddenly becomes quiet. It's a loud roar in my ears as I contemplate where to start. Most of all, how to say what needs to be said and how to go about telling them how a woman struggled for years with the aftershocks of a decision she shouldn't have had to make. My chest tightens. A low rumble emerges from my gut and tension invades the air around us.

"I've been a complete dick to all of you about this over the years, and yet here you are still showing me that you'll always have my back. I owe you all an apology. I'm sorry." I drag my eyes to each one of them, so they can see the truth behind my words, the meaning behind my eyes, and that everything I say from here on out has been bottled up for so long that it's killing me to admit it.

One thing I've always been is a man who believes in eye contact when he speaks. It shows respect, and I have it in spades for these men.

"There's no need. We all care about each other. There's no judgment here, Tyson." No, there isn't, and there never will be.

"I know, Riddick, and I appreciate it. My life was fucked since the day I was born. Lynne was the first person to give me a glimmer of hope. When she left me, I became someone I didn't recognize. When I met you guys, I knew I had a family for life. You helped me through the hardest part of my life by just being there. I was fucked up. A loose cannon. And one day, when we were in the desert, I thought to myself, 'Take a look at Riddick, man. His girl died and even though it gutted him, he's still over there smiling.' I tried. Lord knows I did. I just couldn't get past what she had done. I'm still struggling with it. I may struggle for the rest of my life. Who knows." I take a drag of my cigar, blow out the smoke, and continue. "When we came back from the war, I looked her up. She got married, and that fucked me up even more. Ripped my chest open and tore my heart out. I wanted to destroy her. So, I investigated her family to try and find something on them. Anything to make her pay. The need to know why she left me ate away until I couldn't take it anymore. What I found out nearly killed me. Lynne had cancer. That's one of the reasons why she left me."

"What?" Jude leans forward; his one-syllable word is the same thing I said to myself when I broke into her father's office years ago and found a file with her name on it stashed all the way in the back of a filing cabinet. I dropped to my knees in tears after flipping through all those pages of medical jargon I barely understood. Cancer and hysterectomy were the only two words that stood out.

"I knew right then and there I didn't have it in me to destroy her. She can't have kids. Lynne had a full hysterectomy. She confessed that she left me because of it. Thought I wouldn't stand by her side. The not so funny thing is, I would have never left her because she couldn't have my child. I'm not wired that way. I loved her. Christ, I always have." My hand grips tightly around the bottle of beer. Uncontrolled anger is rippling through me. A tsunami. Tidal wave. Destruction.

"Is she alright? Is her cancer back? Is that why she's back here. To make peace?" Jude enquires.

Riddick and Dane slide their bodies forward. Aligning perfectly with Jude's. The silence has resolved itself to a dull thud around our small table as they wait out my answer.

"You said one of the reasons. What's the other?" Riddick glances down to the tainted file as if he knows it has to do with her father. He's spot on.

"She's cancer free. Has been since she had surgery. Look, I don't want to share the things she and I talked about. It's her private life.

Lynne is here for me. We have a road full of recovery to travel on. It's going to be hard as fuck, but I'm willing to give it a try. This right here"—I signal my head down toward the file—"Him. Her dirty fucking father, he's the other reason why we didn't get married." It's essential that I remain in control over this. The likelihood of me flying off the handle has beaten my odds a time or two. This has to be handled with care. Meticulousness, or he'll find out I know before I'm ready. Maybe I want him to know. To see him fidget in my grasp. Rattle his cage a bit while I decide how far I want to go with this information.

"Tyson, what the hell did he do?" Dane speaks first. I consider what Richard Chapman did to Cora, how he failed to protect an innocent girl when I know without a shadow of a doubt that motherfucker knew her brother was behind the killing of her parents. He had to have known, or at the least expected it.

"It's not about what he did to me; it's what he did to his own daughter. How he took the tragedy of her illness, her mental state, and twisted it to his advantage." I look each one of them square in the eye again for several drawn-out seconds before I spend the next half hour exposing everything that man and his wife did to their own daughter when she needed them to be her parents. But, most of all, she needed me.

"Jesus Christ. I knew that fucker was slime the minute I met him. How in the fuck could he make his daughter give up on the two of you like that? He purposely hurt her." He did a hell of a lot more than that. He wrecked her. Well, I have the answer, and it will piss them off even more.

I tilt my bottle in Riddick's direction and reply.

"Who the fuck knows his reason why. I'm sure her mother had her hands in it as well. That woman is a viper. They both left her alone to deal with the aftermath of what she lost. The very next day, they flew home. They didn't console her, fight with her through any of it. I want her mother checked out. We'll start on her after we deal with this."

"Jesus Christ. I can't even imagine how she must have felt. For fuck's sake." Riddick closes his eyes; when he opens them, there's a slow-burning fire igniting behind them.

"I could use your help. I just need to make sure you're both up for this. You just got married, and you have a teenager to raise. Not taking my chances on anyone getting hurt." Richard has never come at me with violence before. Who the hell knows what he will do when I drop this in his lap. He may try to pull the trigger himself. I need Jude's computer knowledge and Riddick to watch everyone's back.

"Positive," they both respond in unison.

"I'm going to bring in Dominic. You know that big fucker is always putting down for a fight. He'll tail Richard. See what else he's hiding," Dane adds, already reaching into his pocket for his phone.

"You sure? Not going to twist anyone's arm or anything?" I ask, followed by a deep chuckle, knowing full well what their answer will be.

"Hell, yeah, we're sure. You take care of this. I'll keep my eye on Lynne," Riddick says, reaches over, and grips my shoulder.

"I'll keep digging around, see if there's a way to hack into his personal email. After all, it's a criminal investigation, right?" he adds with a slight smirk. It isn't, but who the hell cares at this point. Not like we haven't bent the rulebook before.

"Thanks. It means a lot to me," I say, struggling hard to fight back an emotion new to me. Gratitude.

"You need a lift?"

"I got him," Dane says. Neither he nor Jude had a thing to drink. Jude, I see why he's pretty much stopped. He has Theo, who looks up to him in the highest regards. Can't blame him at all for wanting to set a good example for his kid. Dane, I'm not sure what's going on with him. He's never been one to not want to knock back a few beers and relax.

"We'll talk later. Let us know how you want to handle this." I let out that uncontrolled breath after we pay our tabs and hit the late evening air. The urge to beat the hell out of someone creeps out of every crevice in the sidewalk.

"I will," I respond to the guys through gritted teeth. This trying to remain calm is far from easy. I need to set about doing this the right way. There are innocent people involved who make this a hell of a lot harder to seek out a proper punishment for this crazy fuck I hate with every fiber in my body.

Another thing that has me wound up tight as we all climb into truck similar to each other's is the fact that Riddick and Jude are headed home to their families. It pisses me off even more that I'm traveling in the opposite direction. Back to an empty apartment. And there isn't a damn thing I can do about it. I could grab a bottle and drink, fuck my insecurities away. Neither one of them appeals to me anymore. Not when the object of my desire is so close to me I can taste her.

Fuck, all of this information is going to break her all over again. There has to be a way to get through to her father before all hell breaks loose. I couldn't care less what it does to the rest of her family, but Lynne, she doesn't deserve this. Although, it wouldn't surprise me one bit if Ellen doesn't already know. She's a nosey fucking bitch. Dumber than a two by four to put up with a man like this. Nevertheless, she's a cunt who deserves it.

"Tyson, you need to be sure about this," Dane barks out, breaking through my troubling thoughts.

"I've never been surer in my life. Everything I've wanted has been stolen from me. That fucker took it and wiped his ass with it. He's in over his Goddamn head with this. How he's kept it hidden for this long beats the hell out of us all, Dane. It's time he pays. I'll deal with how this will affect Lynne if she's who you're worried about." I leer a penetrating stare his way, trying to decipher where exactly he's going with this. Not once has Dane questioned anything we've involved him in; he grabs the shit by the balls the same way we do and jerks those fuckers off. He's brutal when he attacks. Something is eating away at him. I know it.

His shadowed jaw ticks slightly under the dashboard lights of his truck and disappears when he turns down my darkened street. He shocks the fuck out of me when he slips into a parking spot and glances my way. The low tone of his voice is quietening my thoughts, stabbing my throat, and piercing my gut. Shit. What the hell happened to him?

"Not too many people know this story. Dominic and I never talk about it. Not even to each other." He pauses, grips the steering wheel tight, and slices me open when I catch a shiny glimmer in his eyes. "Diana, our sister. She killed herself eight years ago after she found out her husband had been cheating on her. My sister wanted kids in a bad way. She pretty much raised Dominic and me. At the time, our parents were married to their jobs. Wanting to set a good example and all that. Anyway, that's beside the point. My point is, Frankie, her husband, told her he didn't want them. Of course, the spineless dick married her first before he let loose that piece of information. She learned to accept it, because she loved the fucker. It wasn't until this woman, the one he had been cheating with, knocked on my sister's door with two little boys. Those boys were Frankie's kids. They're married now, while my sister's remains are in the cold dirt. He ruined her." What in the ever-loving hell?

"Jesus, Dane. I'm sorry, man." What the fuck is wrong with people? Men and women cheating and shit. Don't they give a fuck what it does to the person on the receiving end? Fuck.

"I am, too. I'm telling you this, because I've seen you self-destruct many times. Now that you have Lynne back in your life, make sure you handle this in the right way. She may have told you she doesn't want anything to do with her family, but fuck, Tyson. What we know could shatter her. People can spend a long time in a transitional period. Walking around half empty, always wondering if they'd be full if things would have been done differently. There is no coming back when your life is wrecked. This information is a wreck waiting to happen." He says this as if he's trying to convince himself more than me. To ease his guilty conscience for not being able to help his sister.

"I hear you, Dane. The only thing holding me back from tossing this information in the trash is that this is her father and not her husband. You don't know him like I do. He isn't going to sit around and allow the two of us to be together. He'll fight her. I'll figure out a way to tell her about this. You, on the other hand, should step back from this. I'm so damn sorry about your sister. I would have never asked you to help me out if I knew this was going to pour salt in your wound. Fuck, I never even knew you guys would find information like this. I was looking for corruption, for lies to destroy his career. Not this, never something as bad as this." The right to defend myself is all I've got to give him. I feel guilty as hell for sitting here spewing out words that I hope he understands.

"You have nothing to feel guilty about. It's him, her father. It's Frankie. Those two are the ones to blame. I'm not backing off from helping you out. I may be invested now for my own private vendetta. I couldn't help my sister, because she kept her pain hidden. But I can help you, help Lynne, and protect the innocent." I eye him suspiciously. Dane is a good guy. He's followed through with us many times. I need to be sure he can handle this.

"Don't deny me or Dominic this. It may help us heal." The minute he speaks is the minute I know exactly what we need to do. "Then let's go pay him a visit, shall we? Turn the truck around. We're heading to LA."

***

"You tell your boss if he doesn't see us now, I'll have a search order in my hands within the hour." I'm losing my patience with this woman standing behind this fancy desk with an attitude about as ugly as her personality. Richard sure knows how to pick 'em. Straight off the bitch block.

I ran into my apartment last night. Grabbed a change of clothes and everything I needed for this hostile little visit. Dane did the same, and we drove the short distance to LA, where we found a hotel for the night. Plotted. And now this bitch, who I remember so well from the interrogation involving Cora's brother, is denying me to see him. She was fucking him then. I know for a fact. She probably still is, and I'll rain hell's balls of fire on her if she thinks for one Goddamn second she can keep me away. I have no doubt everyone in this lavish-as-fuck office was told to keep me out. He knows I'm gunning for him. I am. Just not for the reason he thinks.

"Do not pick up that phone," she belts out at the red-headed timid secretary who keeps looking back and forth between the two of us, then keeps her sight trained on me.

"You think that scares me?" The snarly bitch raises her voice even more. Leans her body over the desk to intimidate me. What a smelly worthless piece of shit. She literally stinks with her deceit.

"If it doesn't now, it will when I expose the two of you. I'm not fucking around here, bitch. Either you pick up that phone, or I'll have your ass spread all over the news tonight instead of all over your boss' desk. Something tells me you don't want that."

I give a friendly little wink to the secretary when she gasps so loud that this bloodhound's fangs hang out.

"Fuck you," she snarls, her face turning red. Her eyes begin to bug out of her resting bitch face head.

"No, thanks. Not after you've been fucking him." The secretary laughs. I hope to God the people milling about this place heard me. Every damn one of them.

"How dare you. Haven't you done enough to his family?" Her voice lowers to a mere whisper. I have never wanted to punch a woman as much as I do her. Not even Lynne's mom. This chick is a straight up cunt.

"Not even close. I'm only beginning, sweetheart. Pull up a Goddamn chair and watch."

"My God, he was right about you."

"Probably. Don't really care what he thinks of me. Last chance, sweetheart. You do not get a warning bell here. No time-outs. No breaks. You tell him I'm here, or I'm planting your ass firmly in one of those chairs, cuff you to it, and it will not be for pleasure." I point to a row of chairs stationed against the wall behind me.

"What the hell is going on out here?"

"Well, what do you know? It's the asshole subject of this conversation. You want me to say what I came for out here or in private? It's up to you." I take the few steps needed to reach Richard. Dane is right behind me. Fuck, he's is one ugly son of a bitch. How the hell he produced a woman as beautiful as Lynne I'll never know.

"Hold all my calls. If you value your job, you'll keep your mouth shut." He lifts his arm, points it in the direction of his secretary, and snarls.

"Fuck him; you want a job, call me. I'll treat you a hell of a lot better than this fucker does." I grin at Dane's comment, crane my neck to make sure the cute little secretary is alright, and laugh when he pulls a business card from his wallet and hands it to her.

"I may do that," she says with a devious smile. I love her already.

"You'll never work in this town again," I hear the bitch say before Richard slams the door and locks it. Something tells me the redhead doesn't even care.

"Damn. I think you lost a secretary, Dick. How's the house?" He doesn't respond. He can't. Not when the hostility in this room is set at a hundred degrees. It's palpable. Ricocheting off his walls, shining from the glass on his windows, and smacking him upside his head.

"You have five minutes, you little motherfucker. Or I'm calling the cops."

"Five minutes. That's more than you gave your daughter." I toss the file on his desk. "I'm ready to burn you alive, Richard. There isn't a cop in this state, a judge in your pocket that can save your ass from the information inside of there. Dare to take a guess at what I found out? I'll bet my life you're hiding a lot more than this. You screwed with the wrong guy. Revenge is a tricky motherfucker, Richard, and it's finally walked through your door."

CHAPTER EIGHT

LYNNE

I set my phone down on my desk and close my eyes. I've lost count of the times I've done that over the past few days. My heart is begging to hear his voice. My mind is telling me to allow him time to absorb while it drifts off trying to figure out a way to tie the remaining loose ends of my life.

The whittling weight on my shoulders decreased in abundance after letting things go the other night with Tyson. It's a strange emotional drain lifted, and I'm swimming in its warmth.

We shifted into a good place when I bared my soul, bled my words, and shed my skin in front of him. I felt so exposed that it hurt as much to be in his company as it did for me to speak the truth. It was all wiped out when he scooped me up and made contact with his sentimental green-filled eyes. His words were like dripping off pages of a fairytale. He caressed my skin, stole my breath, and left me emotionally paralyzed with a traffic jam out of nowhere in my head. All of it came to a complete stop in an instant.

I don't feel guilt, shame, or blame anymore. Those coldly targeted uproars that have stirred in my body for as long as I can remember have been rubbed away by an invisible eraser. Only the faintest mark can be seen.

Will I always own up to being weak? For not demanding my rights, for not sticking up for a man who stumbled through the gates of hell to find me. Yes, yes, I will. I won't lie. It's beneath me to do so anymore. A part of me will always suffer for taking his love for granted. For listening to my parents and tuning the entire world out.

It's time for me to listen. To allow the same phrase my therapist told me over and over again, and yet I never allowed it to sink in, to shine as brightly as the sweltering sun. Tyson drilled it into me with his touch, his truth to me to forgive myself for the cruel punishment I conflicted on a man who didn't deserve it. I broke his heart, and if he's willing to try and forgive me, then so can I.

We've suffered for far too long, and now it's time to process this and move forward. To plant a new seed and watch it grow without the pesky weeds getting in the way. *Together*, he said.

I open my eyes, swiping a lonely tear from my cheek. My chest feels warm as it slowly liquefies to the philosophy of my life. In an instant, it stops, threatens to freeze right back up. To seize hold of my thoughts and weaken my state of mind when I think of my family. They aren't going to walk away from this. Not a chance in hell will they allow me to live a normal, happy life. Not when they are all miserable in their own selfish ways. I've thought so much about my parents and sisters over these past few days that I've come to the conclusion that I should have cut the imaginative umbilical cord that's been choking me since the day I was born.

For reasons I may never know, I clung to an already dead theory of hope that once I stood on my own two feet, they would change. It will never happen. My parents and my sisters' unanswered emails, voice mails, and text messages I've deleted have proven it. All of them think I'm slipping back into depression. That I need help again to overcome some sick obsession I have with a man who in their words isn't good enough for me. Even Larissa has changed her tune from the other day. I knew it was all a lie. My mother sunk her fangs into her and dripped venom into her mind. I hate them all.

"I don't care who you are. I will not let you barge in there." Maggie startles me with her anger-pitched voice. Clearing my head and bringing me back to what's happening outside of my closed office door. I have rarely heard her yell, let alone raise her tone in a lethal filled. Not in the way that has me righting from my chair and bolting for my door to see what the hell is going on.

"Who do you think you are speaking to me that way? I'm her mother. I have more right to be here than you do. You're nothing but a lowly secretary. Now, let me past. I want to see my daughter." Oh no, she did not just turn her nose down on my friend. I should have known she would eventually show up here. I've been avoiding every form of communication from all of those poison-filled people.

"I'll tell you who I am. I'm the lowly secretary who's going to knock you flat on your ass, drag you out of here by the hair on your head, and toss you on the dirty sidewalk. Now, you will march your snobby little ass back to the waiting room as instructed and wait." My hand flies over my mouth to stifle the laugh that rightfully wants to escape. My mother deserved that, and I'd love to see it happen. Maggie, however, does not deserve to fight my battles regardless of how much she despises my mother.

Even if it wipes me clean of the inheritance my grandparents left me, I'll gladly give it to Maggie for defending me from the wrath of this wicked woman who is truly showing how vindictive she is.

I swing open the door. Anger erupts when I stare into a face similar to my own. "Mother, if you ever show up here and talk to my friend in that way again, I will call the cops on you. We both know that is a scandal you surely don't want." Shit. I need to tell Tyson about what I've been doing since I found something out about my father. I wonder what he'll think. *You should clue him in on all of it.* I'll go see him tonight and tell him everything.

"Well, if you had returned our calls, then I wouldn't have had Stewart drive me here, now would I? What in the world is going on with you, Lynne? Surely, it's hanging around with people like her." She brushes past Maggie as if she owns this place. Marching her snobbish, stinking bullshit, her expensive suit, and the strong whiff of her Chanel perfume lingering in the air right into my office. Poor Stewart most likely had to listen to her complain all the way here.

"What a bitch. My God, if she weren't your mother, I would fuck her up. This place is going to need an exterminator after she leaves,"

Maggie expresses, her nostrils flaring.

"You can call them now if you'd like." I wind an arm around her slender waist for a hug. "I'm sorry. I love you so much," I say truthfully. I've apologized for my mother's behavior over the years more times than I can count. From teachers to my school, to telling the nurses at the hospital to call her every day when I was sick, because the minute she and my father found out all my cancer was gone, they left. Figured they had stuck by my side long enough. They didn't care that once my incision had healed enough, I had chemo to go through just to be sure. It was awful. I wretched my guts out. Cried for Tyson and relied on strangers to clean me up. There has never been a day in my life when I can remember my mother not being a full-fledged bitch.

"I'm not sorry. She's a snobby old hag who can't see what a wonderful child she has, because her head is shoved up her stinky ass. This door is staying open." Maggie's words bounce off the walls. If only they would smack my mother on her ass and drop her to the ground, then all would be right in my world.

I stifle back my laugh. "That she is. Give me a few minutes to see what she wants, and then we'll be out of here," I say, untangling my arms from around her. She's been my comfort zone, an escape to reality for long enough. It's time for me to put my mother in her place. To prove to myself I can do it.

"Make sure you tell her to fuck right off."

"I'm going to tell her more than that." I shift my gaze from her troubled eyes to the woman standing behind me. A woman I barely recognize.

"Shut the door," my mother says in her nasty, nasally voice.

"I'm closing it not because you're telling me to but because I do not want Maggie to hear what I have to say to you. Who in the hell do you think you are?" I wait for Maggie to go back to doing whatever she was doing before she was rudely interrupted, and slam the door, making Ellen Chapman jump.

"I'm your mother. That's who I am. You've been avoiding all of our calls. This has gone on long enough. You cannot shut us out of your life. We're your family." I bellow out my laugh over her remark. How delusional can she be? Blinders. All of them.

"Really, mother. I haven't been avoiding you. I don't want to talk to you. There's a big difference there. And you are not my family," I jab. "I don't think you know the meaning of the word. None of you do. You show up here on my turf, in my office, and call my friend lowly. She is far from lowly, and she has a name. It's Maggie. That woman out there has been more of a mother to me than you have my entire life. Now, get the hell out of my office and don't come back. I'm through with all of you." I grin so hard in triumph it nearly cracks my face. That is until she stalks toward me with feral eyes, her palm rising up to slap my face. I catch it mid-air. A form of determination is controlling my bitterness toward this hateful woman.

"Let go of me, you ungrateful little twat." I jerk her harder. My fingers are wrapping tightly around her wrist to the point it smarts my hand. I'm not about to let up, though. I want her to see the mark. To leave a reminder that I mean it this time.

"Come on now, mother. Surely, you can do better than twat? Nuisance. Pest. Troublesome. Those words fit your description of me better, don't they? Now, you listen to me. What I have to say you can take right back to my arrogant father. To the farce of a marriage you have. To my sisters. Everyone in your Goddamn circle. I'm tired of all of you meddling in my life. You are a twisted, sick bitch who helped destroy a relationship with the man I loved. You should have been there for me, mother. He should have been there with me." I'm breathing so hard I feel faint. It doesn't stop me from tugging her to within an inch of my face. God, how I would love to spit all over her. She would really think I've lost my mind if I did.

"You need help," she whispers. I honestly think she means what she's saying.

"If I do, it won't be coming from you. Not a damn one of you. One would guess your lives would be easier without meddling in mine. You allowed me to grieve for children I will never have. I needed you to hold me. To tell me I was going to be alright. Not a one of you stopped to think that what happened to me ripped away a part of me I will never get back. The part of me that was most loved. Him. You stole years from us. You tormented me and broke my heart. It's taken this long for me to find the courage to say I hate you. I will never forgive any of you for hurting him and me the way you did. I'm not your daughter anymore. For the last time, get your filthy, stinky ass out of my office. And I swear on my grandmother's grave that if you contact me or any of you come near Tyson, I will not hesitate for one minute to have a sit down with any reporter for free to tell them all about the many indiscretions both you and my father have tried to hide. Do I make myself clear?" I release my hold on her. Step back and open the door.

I'm sweating, shaking, and I want her out of here.

Except she's not done. She fires me a disgusting glare. I should have known better than to think she would waltz out of here without digging her words into my healed flesh, slicing me with words she hopes will never repair me.

"You will do no such thing. Our personal lives will remain just that. I'm your mother; it's not your right to know my business; it's my right to know yours. Don't you see he's not right for you? How many times did we tell you this? He's nothing but a drunk, a mishap of a man. He's a whore, Lynne. Is that the kind of man you want?" Her eyes flare angrily at her unwanted admission. If I had it in me, I would hit her so hard she would fall on her surgically lifted ass.

"Oh, my God. Your rights? You have none when it comes to me. Zero. And I would never dream of living a life like yours, mother. What he has done while we weren't together is none of my business. You saw to that. It's what he's doing now that means something to me." She is not going to try and get me to admit I know more about their business than I'm letting on. It's quite funny to me. She has all but admitted she knows. I knew it. She's kept this secret, too. How could she do this? "You've been keeping tabs on Tyson, haven't you? You really are a shallow woman. I'm not surprised about this at all. You can't see past your own feet to realize I do not care what he has done in the past. It was you and your corruption to me that drove him to do those things. You took him away from me. Tainted my mind when I had no idea if I was going to live or die. How can you stand there and inject your hatred toward the things my father has done to you into me? How can you not see that all I ever wanted was Tyson? If you were any kind of a decent human, you would have left that bastard years ago. Erased his poison from your mind and raised your children in an environment full of love, not hate, cheating, and full of lies. God forbid that Ellen Chapman would want to be happy. So what does she do? She enthralls her misery on her daughter. Takes the knife and shoves it in. Never mind the fact her child was suffering from cancer. From finding out she will never be able to carry a child of her own, because everything she thought she wanted was ripped right out of her body. Tyson loved me, mother, and we are going to make this work. You make me sick. GET OUT!" I do not want to continue this conversation. I'm done transgressing back to what happened to me. I have a chance at happiness with Tyson. She is not going to touch that again.

I don't want her touching me when she stoically stands there and hikes her purse on her shoulder. I pull the door open as far as it will go, my body trailing along with it. Glaring at her as she struts in her heels toward the door, where I'm still holding solidly to the knob, afraid to let go because I want to slap her. Knock her on her cold, hard ass and stomp on her turned-up face. Possibly beat her bloody with my fists.

"Your father won't approve of this." I loathe that she's right about him. He won't give up. He'll damn me to hell. Dig and fester until his littered mind voices he's won. I have no reservations about pushing him away this time if he comes charging at me like a raging bull. I'll lasso his ass and stomp him to the ground, too. I'm not backing away from the man I love. Not this time. And I'm not going to stand here and give her the ammunition to use to try and do so. They can continue on their own. Create a global witch hunt for all I care. They won't burn me this time. I simply won't allow it. Tyson won't either.

"I don't give a fuck what he approves or disapproves of. You either. Last warning. Get out, or I'm calling the police," I sneer. Her head jerks back as if I've slapped her. I hope it stings. Burns. Festers and falls off her neck. God, how I wish my palm was smarting an angry shade of red right now. She deserves it and so much more.

"What has happened to you? You were fine after your treatments. You found Robert. Surely, you can find someone else. Why him? Why?"

"No. You do not get to play the role of being my mother. Not know. Not ever."

"I am your mother, Lynne. There isn't a thing you can do to change that," she whimpers.

"Wrong again." She's testing my patience and years of training to hold my tongue.

"You need to go," I say calmly.

"This isn't over. You'll need me. I know you will."

"I will never need you. Not ever," I dare to say as she glides right past me in her self-righteous glory.

I take a much-needed breath while following her down the hall, my gaze dragging to Maggie the minute the door slams shut, leaving a foul smell in the air. Maybe we really should call an exterminator.

"Are you okay?" She examines my composure for internal bruising before she bursts out laughing, evoking a loud sprinkle of the same from me.

"She is heartless." I titter, trying to gain some self-control before I collapse to the floor. On the outside, I'm showing no fear. On the inside, I'm scared to death. I've provoked the devil in her. She'll run right back to my father and twist what I said. She'll lie to get her own way and make shit up. That's how she is. A contorted figure of pure animosity to make anyone who doesn't agree with her miserable.

"I'm proud of you. You should be proud of yourself. For God's sake, Lynne. How you put up with her for all these years is beyond me. You are so much stronger than you give yourself credit for." I used them, that's how.

"Tyson said the same thing to me the other night. I didn't believe it wholeheartedly until she showed up. It's far from over, though. Trust me when I say she's the gust of wind before the hurricane strikes."

"Well, he can bring his best game. I'll be damned if I'll let either one of them try to drag you down. You've come too far. Do you remember when we met? How you stood close enough to hear me but far enough away that I had to keep the kids close to shore?"

I nod my head. All laughter gone as her face turns serious and her speech resembles a caring, doting mother. All I could see when she strolled onto the beach were her grandchildren. Two little boys who have a grandmother who adores them. A family. I never really knew my grandparents. They lived in London. Family vacations or visiting them weren't important to my parents. I met them twice when I was almost too young to remember. When they both died within a year of each other, all three of us girls were shocked they had cut my mother out of their will and left millions to each of us and our uncle.

"I do too. I watched you out of the corner of my eye. You stood there answering my questions and not once did you take your concentration off of watching my grandchildren. You were mesmerized by them. I knew then you were hurting. Your eyes told me that something inside of you died. Days later, when you sat on the beach with us, you moved closer to me. Within my reach. You told me everything that day. You trusted a stranger. I heard what you said to her about me being more than just your secretary. I want you to know I feel the same way about you. I love you, Lynne. It doesn't take a woman to give birth to a child to be their mother. It takes a woman strong enough to move heaven and earth to protect them. A woman who would give their own life to ensure they are happy. You can be that woman, sweetheart. You have to do what we talked about."

My chest stills. Her point of view means the world to me.

"I don't know if I can."

"Yes, you can. It's up to you to take my advice and run with it."

I press an open palm to my stomach. Confidence flutters its wings and rises to my throat. This is what I wanted to talk to Tyson about. I need to do it. I can do anything. All I have to do is try.

CHAPTER NINE

TYSON

Richard smiles, chuckling in the same way he did years ago when I told him to fuck off and choke on his money. He fails to forget I've dealt with far worse pieces of shit than he is and his patronizing full-of-himself courtroom bullshit isn't going to work on me.

"My place is to protect my daughter from people such as you. If you show her this, it will devastate her. You've already manipulated her against us by not staying away from her. Haven't you done enough?" He closes the file without glancing at the photos, sits his ass on the corner of his desk, and crosses his arms.

"That's the same thing your little slut out there asked me. I'll be a little more direct with you than I was with her. You are nothing but a fucking maggot. A man I'm going to ruin. I'm bending and this close to snapping with the haven't-I-done-enough bullshit." I pinch my thumb and index finger together. It balls up in a tight fist before it drops to my side. I'm waiting on some kind of unanswered prayer he says something to piss me off so I can use it.

"I'm on a roll now, motherfucker. I'll tell you the same thing I told that bitch out there. I've only begun to show you how much enough is. As far as you protecting her, what kind of delusional world are you living in? Jesus. I know everything, you dumb fuck, and you have the balls to actually stand there and speak to me as if you've done nothing wrong? The daughter you claim to protect had cancer, and instead of allowing me to take care of her, you left her to strangers clear across the country. That isn't protecting your child to me. That's destroying her Goddamn life. I'm not here because you persuaded her to leave me. This isn't about that. It's about you crushing her heart when she needed you the most." Despite how badly I want to choke the life out of him, I'm not going to lay a hand on him today. For once, I'm going to play this all out the right way. Protect the innocent and persecute the guilty like I've been taught.

"She needed treatment, looked after. We gave that to her." I stand there in a maddening craze. Fumes are billowing out of my ears over what he just said. My heartbeat is thrashing roughly inside of my chest. My head is aching over how I'm going to tell her this. It's all too much.

"She needed me," I raise my voice.

"How would you have helped her when you would have been gone? She would have had to worry about you on top of worrying about herself."

"She would have been my wife. I would never have left her side."

"And the Army? War? I suppose you would have walked away from that, too," he scoffs.

"Goddamn right, I would have. There wouldn't have been a damn thing that would have stopped me."

"You and I both know that isn't true. Once you sign, the government owns you. My daughter would have been left on some base being looked after by kids who can barely wipe their ass. She's fine. Healthy. Who the hell knows where she would be if I had allowed her to marry you." He sits there gloating. Acting as if his daughter's life was a game and he had won. Every time he opens his mouth, I feel the heat down my back from the anger rolling off Dane. If I don't move us along, finish this up, then he's going to fly from behind me and do his worst on this fucking bastard.

"Jesus, Richard. Listen to yourself. Does Lynne mean so little to you that she couldn't have been taken care of here? That what she really needed was to have someone who loved her hold her when she was sick, afraid? You sent her away to keep her from me. That right there isn't looking after her. That's mutilated hatred for me and for her. You sent your daughter to be slaughtered, and she survived. I'm going to watch you burn, Richard. I'm going to hit you below your belt and crush you underneath my palm. You stay the fuck away from her. Lynne is no longer your concern. She's mine. She deserves to have everything, and I'm going to give it to her. You can keep that file. Take a good hard look at those photos inside and trust me when I say I'm telling her everything." I cock my head mockingly while I wait for him to give me more ammunition to kill him with. He knows as well as I do that the information I have on him isn't illegal. It's not going to extinguish him in the way I wish it could. What it will do is snuff out the torch he carries in this town. Damage his reputation beyond repair.

"You tell her, and it will—" I grab him by his raunchy little throat. Fuck the no-touching rule. He will not patronize me. He will not toss any part of her in my face.

"It will what? Make her see you for who you really are? She already knows. I'm done here. This was a warning. Take it back to your wife, your daughters, and all of you fuck right off. You come near her, and the reporters get that." I shove him backward, point to the folder behind him. It's bright green color tempting me to pick it up and head straight for the news station.

"Your five minutes are up. Get out."

"Will do. Just so you remember. I'm just beginning to turn into the unforgiving savage that's been gnawing at my soul. You better pray to God that's the only thing you're hiding." I shift my stance toward the door, walk out satisfied in the God given fact I'm going to be the death of that man. All I need to do now is figure out how to tell Lynne first.

***

I've spent the last half hour sitting in the parking lot waiting for Lynne to exit her office.

After Dane and I walked out of Richard's office and calmed the fuck down, this is all we talked about. How I was going to tell her. Lay it on her gently and pray it wouldn't hurt her. She's so much stronger than she realizes. Possibly more than I realize. If this sets her back, she'll never be able to forgive herself.

I refuse to start our newfound relationship off with secrets and lies. There will be no half-truths here, no rummaging around to save her from the pain. I have to spit it out. Get it over with and show her I'm not going anywhere.

I close my eyes, tilt my head back, and rest. At the moment, there isn't any comfort or relief over having Lynne back in my life. Not after learning about this. Not after seeing her father determined to tear her down even more.

I jump from the light tap on my window, my hand automatically reaching for my gun. Christ. I need a good night's rest. Being jumpy is not good.

"Tyson. Is everything alright?" Big green, luminous eyes filled with worry stare back at me. Eyes I could look into for days. Damn. She gets more beautiful every time I see her.

I roll down my window. Gut turning in turmoil. Head spinning and a long road of regret sitting in the pit of my stomach. "It is now. How's it going, Maggie?" I take my eyes off the intoxicating woman standing close to my rolled down window to seek out her neighbor. I'll chicken the hell out if I continue to look at her. I'm breaking under this ironclad wired façade once again. This time, it's out of protection. It's a sad day when you know you're going to unintentionally stomp on someone's heart from the wrongdoings of her father.

"I'm good. You're just what she needs. I'll see you tomorrow, dear."

My brows deepen wondering what Maggie means. I'll put my gun to use if her father has contacted her. Prison or not, I'll kill him.

"I guess I need a ride home." She shrugs casually.

"Hop in. I was hoping to catch you anyway," I say, roll up my window, and allow her to capture my attention. Each time I see her, it gets harder not to pull her into my arms and brush my lips across hers. Not innocently either. It would be fired up with a requisite to strip her out of that tight little skirt. To hike it up over her thighs and shred her bare. Get a glimpse of her sweet little pussy.

There isn't a chance in hell I'm going to be gentle with her once I have her naked and in bed. Not a Goddamn chance. The way I see it, she doesn't need gentle anymore. Lynne isn't as fragile as people have made her believe she is. Not after the life she's led. Not after living with the bloodthirstiness of a family out to turn her into someone she isn't.

"Tell me what you meant when you said 'better now.' Did something bad happen at work?" she queries, hikes herself up in my truck, and gazes hungrily up and down my body. A deep, heavy sigh escapes her mouth and shoots straight to my dick. I can't answer. Not when the woman I've dreamt about for years is sitting in the cab of my new truck, her presence alone making me fall all over again. Everything about her has me trapped between common sense and practicality.

Sexual tension is a livewire in this truck. It's flickering. Igniting and curling around the base of my spine. Tapping into my brain to get closer to the one beautiful thing in my life.

Admiringly, I switch to observe the slant of her eyes, the slope of her neck, the increasing rise and fall of her chest, all the way down and back up again. Christ. Beauty is all around her.

When her eyes latch onto mine and a whimper escapes her lips, I lose control. It's been a long time coming, and if I don't drown myself in the taste of this strong, strong woman first, I'll never make it through this. I need her.

Unclipping my seatbelt, I lunge for her as if I were a man released from prison. In a way, I have been. Bound to chains tethered to my feet, steel against my wrists, and a vice clamped around my heart.

My hands grip her waist as her eyes turn into shocked circular saucers. I'm fighting the desire gushing through my veins to drag her ass over my rock-hard cock to straddle me. Feel those legs around my hips and rock my erection to the hot flesh between her sexy little thighs.

Instead, I grip the back of her neck, palm the pink flush, her pulse pounding underneath my touch. Fuck, this crazy shiny star looks up to me with all the trust in the world. I want to fuck up her father so damn bad. To hold him hostage and strangle his Goddamn ass. Shoot him as if he were the enemy. He *is* the enemy. A coward. A pathetic excuse to mankind for not seeing the woman she is. For not respecting her enough to see her happy. Follow her wishes and provide her with the kind of love she is worthy of.

"You are so beautiful in every sense of the word. Kind, gentle, and undeserving of anyone who has ever hurt you." She inhales a deep breath, holding it in. I do the only thing I've wanted to do for years when the air from her lungs expels. I draw it in. Strength.

A sizzle fills my truck. She moans, and all the darkness, sensibility, and pain disappear with one swipe of my tongue across her bottom lip. I kiss her. Wild and deep. Frantic and desperate. Our teeth gnash together, tongues dueling in an all-out gritty fight. She tastes like promises left unspoken. A long life without pain. An earth-shattering moment that won't wait.

My dick begs to be set free from the margins of my jeans. I've never had the willpower to let go of her mouth, yet this time I do. There are hurtful things to be said. A reminder lodged in my skull so deep that it grates on my nerves. Dishevels my thoughts with dread. I can't let this bring her down. No one is going to take my right away from me this time to be the protective guard she needs. Strength.

"I've missed you more than you will ever know. I need to talk to you about a few things. Is it all right if we hang at your house for a bit?" I fix my eyes on her. Wild. Crazed. Smiling.

"Yes," she whispers from those tantalizing, swollen lips. God, I'm a selfish fuck for mauling her, giving her hope that what I want is to take her to bed. The craving to do just that bubbles my blood and boils it with a thick, heavy hunger only for her.

It dismisses itself the minute she pulls away from me. My thoughts resume to the complications that could arise from all of this. Will she sink back into depression? Go stark raving mad? Hell, I have no clue what she will do with this information.

"You're scaring me," she reveals after several long minutes of silence.

Out of the corner of my eye, I can see her eyes clenched shut. Her hands planted firmly under her ass and digging into my leather seat.

"Do you trust me?" She scoffs as if my question is a joke to her.

"Of course, I do." I heave in a heavy, loaded breath from her declaration. If only she had trusted me years ago. I tamp that notion down. She had no choice but to put her trust in the two people who brought her into this world. Today, though, she's making a choice on her own. One she should always have the right to make.

Lynne couldn't begin to understand how much hearing her say that means to me. We've been lost for so long that trust shouldn't be here right now. It's a gift from a divine spirit that connected us in the first place. Then ripped us apart as if it didn't matter. Lynne has always made it easy for me to put her first. It's the way it should be when you care for someone. Their needs before your own. Their happiness always before any other. It's what sprouts the definition of trust. I can't live or function without it. Someone to have my back while I take their front. Reverse the roles when the opportunity arises.

"What we're going to talk about has nothing to do with you and me. I found out something you should know about."

Lynne ponders her thoughts. I can see the bare-threaded wheels turning in her head. I'm about to reassure her again, but she beats me to it. In fact, she leaves me staggering.

"I see. Well, there's only one thing I can think it could be. It has to do with my father, doesn't it? You know, Tyson, don't you?"

CHAPTER TEN

LYNNE

"How long have you known?" he huffs out in frustration. My eyes fill with tears, and I stare straight out the window with a deep ache in my chest. A whirlwind of turmoil swirling inside of me. My inability to form words leaves me breathless. This man isn't going to give up when it comes to burning my father's bridges to the ground. This is one he has to leave alone. I simply won't allow it.

"Five years," I lead, catching my breath and wondering if I should carry on or wait the couple of minutes or so it will take to get to my home.

I haven't told anyone but Maggie about this. My intentions were to tell him everything tonight. He's beaten me to it. How true it is that Tyson and I seem to be on the same wave of destroying my father? Except I have others to protect. I hope he can see that. Understand everything I'm about to tell him.

"And you know where they are?" His voice rises an octave. He's angry.

"I do." My resolve starts slipping. A tear falls from the corner of each eye and travels slowly down the cheeks of my face. One each for the two little boys I've fallen hopelessly in love with.

Except for today, when my mother was digging around, every thrashing hint I've threatened my parents with lately they seem to tune out. Except for today, when my mother came digging. They seem to think they're invincible. I suppose to people like them, they really believe they are. It's obvious that every time I've threatened, they've assumed I've been talking about my father's affairs. A part of me has. But there's a bigger part, the one that led to the birth of my two innocent half-brothers who would not be where they are today if it weren't for the pawning, scheming blackmail that eventually consumed their birth mother's guilt until she took her own life. On behalf of that part, there isn't a chance in hell I will sit back and allow them to live a life without me. My goal is to protect those boys from anyone.

"How much do you know? Do you know that my father did nothing to acknowledge he had two children left without a mother? And that he covered his tracks well in the eyes of the law by making sure his name wasn't on their birth certificate, hid them away, and paid her off to keep her mouth shut until she couldn't take it anymore? She killed herself, Tyson. I blame him for her death. He may as well have poured those pills down her throat himself. I have never been so ashamed to be a man's daughter in all my life. My mother, too. I'll bet my life on it she knows. Those two have created their own Hollywood movie. If I weren't living it, I wouldn't believe it."

"I know everything about her death. What I don't know is how you could hold this in for so long. Jesus, Lynne. I've been beating my head in for two days trying to come up with a way to tell you, and you've known the entire time." I don't miss the angered edge in his tone. It's not aimed at me. It's directed at my father. His disregard. His capability of proving the type of man he truly is.

"I was planning on telling you tonight. I felt we needed closure to our own issues first." Tyson starts his truck, pulls out of the lot, and drives in silence. I glance from the road ahead to the caring man next to me. The muscles in his jaw are ticking and flexing as he presumably contemplates all of this information inside his head.

If he found out about them, then surely he knows where they are. Just when I strum up the words to put his mind at ease, we pull down my street, slide into my driveway, and maneuver out of his truck and into my house. In quietness. I need to know what he's thinking. How he feels. He needs to hear my plans. What I feel is right for those boys before he blows his top and this escalates any further.

"I didn't know they were being moved to a new family here until after I found you. I love them, Tyson. I want them, but I've been frightened to fight against my father. That is"—I say, plucking the folder out of his hand and tossing it on the cushion of one of my chairs. I don't need it. I'm very well acquainted with the lives of Jacob and Joshua Long. Born on Christmas Day in 2008 to one Lori Long. There's more. So much more to reveal about them. It needs to be said aloud. Right now, my focus is the man standing right in front of me. His eyes are showing an unreadable expression—"until you convinced me I can accomplish anything on my own." I hold my breath. Tyson and I, we are so incredibly raw. I know better than anyone how life can change on a whim, how you become so caught up in certain situations that before you know what's happening, you're spiraling out of control. Spinning. I don't want him to think he has to play a part in this at all.

"I'm not sure if I want to kiss the ever-loving fuck out of you or drag your ass over to your couch and spank it." I smile wide out of confusion and lust. A spanking sounds tempting, but I'm not ready for that. Not tonight anyway.

I sigh in submission and will myself to step closer, arms circling around his neck, fingers tangling in the thick hair at the nape. He kissed me earlier. I want him to do it again. All night if he wants. He felt so good, so tempting, and I loved the way he took control of it and surrendered at the same time. One touch, one kiss is all it took to reassure us both that nothing is going to separate us again.

Tyson needs to understand how important these kids are to me, too, and the plans I've thought about setting in motion but always seemed to be stuck in the starting position. Unable to move out of fear. I'm not scared anymore. Tyson convinced me in a matter of hours that I'm strong enough to do anything. It's the courage I crave to tell him more. To pick his brain, dump the loaded question on him. The same one I've been asking myself for years, and with each passing day, I have yet to make the decision to answer it.

"I'll take the kiss," I confess, my voice dripping with the thirst-filled wish only he can possess out of me.

Torture spikes my nerves; patience tempts my heart as Tyson slowly lowers his mouth to mine. Every inch feeling like an eternity. His hands press gently in the back of my hair, rough, calloused fingers yank out of nowhere, and he smirks ever so slightly before his mouth takes hold of mine in a kiss that pushes the air out of my lungs. It steals away the first kiss we shared; it's better than the one from minutes ago. It triumphs over them all. We move close, and we fall apart. Our mouths fused together, they circuit, they combust, and my bones rattle inside my chest. I want to pull away before I lose myself in him. Before this gets carried away. I can't seem to, though; he's seducing my mind with every swipe of his tongue, every brush that lights up my universe and swallows me whole.

"Fuck, woman," he rasps against my tender lips. "You are so full of shit if you honestly believe you are not capable of being strong. I don't think you see the person you are, Lynne. I understand why you haven't exposed your father. The way your face lit up when you told me you wanted those boys was an image I'll never forget. Jesus. Here I thought this news was going to break your heart and instead, you've stunned me. Every word you utter defines the woman you are. So unforgettable. You not only came here for me, but you also came here for those boys. Don't you see where all of this is going? The things we talked about the other night. You amaze me." He looks down at me as if I matter. As if all the words jumbled up in my head, all the ache filling my heart for those boys who are now in a well-rounded home stabilized and secure could be mine.

"If you met them, you would understand so much more. They may have lost their mother, but they are nothing like my father. As far as I know, he's never even met them. They are such good little boys. I see them as much as I can. They have no idea I'm their sister. I don't want them to know. Not yet. I can't bring disruption to their lives like that."

"Goddamn, Lynne. You can't keep something as important as this from them. If they were to find out…"

"I know, alright? I've thought about it all. Every little question, every big challenge. I've thought about it. I've made myself sick over it. I've done it all, Tyson. The one thing I haven't done is tell them. Not until they become mine and are old enough to understand." I step away from him. Not because I want to. It's because we went from kissing to disagreeing in a blink of an eye.

"Does your father know that you know?" Tyson's hard stare nearly wobbles me. I feel my legs go weak while the rest of my body strings up taut.

"No. I found out by accident. I went to make a copy of some papers for school in his office. He left his computer open; it was right there for me to see. All of it. Photos, the mother's death certificate. I made my copies and left. Went to my room and booked the first flight home I could find. I had to think, investigate, and do it when I was alone. I've never told him or my mother. Although, I think they may suspect. Why?" His jaw clenches tight. I can see his pulse throbbing in his neck.

"I paid your father a visit today." I cringe. Feel my knees begin to shake. I move to the couch and sit. Afraid I'll say the wrong thing if I'm close to him. He wants to use this against him. I knew it. This will surely end my dream of ever becoming a mother.

"I was going to ask you not to investigate him. I wish you would have come to me. This could ruin everything. You don't know my father the way I do. He's going to come here, and he'll try to work me over to see if I know. My mother came to visit me today. She was all over my ass about you. I finally told her to fuck off. That I never wanted anything to do with them again. And now this. If he has one inkling in his mind that I want those kids, he'll do everything in his power to send them where I won't be able to find them." I glance up at him. He looks so handsome. So sure of himself, with his arms crossed over his chest. His eyebrows lifted. He's pissed. Well, good. So am I.

On top of the fact I'm a complete idiot for dreaming I could somehow keep this a secret from my family until I asked Tyson my question of helping me find an attorney of my own. Someone who wouldn't be afraid to go up against my father if they had to.

"I would never hurt those innocent kids. I should have talked to you first. But I'll be Goddamned if I'm going to shove my foot up my ass, stand by and watch your parents interfere in our business again. They can go fuck themselves to death. I don't give a shit. I'm not the one you should be pissed off at, and you damn well know it. Fight the son of a bitch if you have to. He isn't above the law. No one is. You have me in your corner now. Jude, Tyson, Dane. Hell, even the girls. There isn't a chance in hell that son of a bitch will come after you. I'll publicly string him by his balls before I let him hurt you again."

"Don't you understand what I'm trying to say? I'm done with lies. Done with seeing people get hurt. Those boys will be in the middle of this."

"Do you want those kids or not?"

"Of course, I do. They mean everything to me."

"Then you fight, Goddamn it. If any of what you just said happens, then you show them the type of woman you really are. You show them that you can be exactly the type of person they wanted you to be. Ruthless and conniving. Powerful. You stand up for what you want, and you fight for them. Don't back down this time. Don't let your family have power over you anymore. You said you were done with them, then you prove it."

I picture my father spattering lies out of his mouth. Tossing me around like the scared little girl he assumes me to be. I know he'll come knocking on my door sooner than later. He'll create havoc, turn my life upside down in order to get me to cave the same way I did years ago. Except now he has another reason to gash open my scars. Two beautiful, innocent reasons.

"I don't want to fight with you over this. I've been jumping over hurdles for years to avoid conflict with him. All I've done was pretend to care about all of them. I'm not afraid of him anymore. What I am afraid of is that the hatred he has for you is stronger than his love for anything. He'll lie his bloodthirsty head off to seek revenge on you. He has the money, the power to claim he didn't know about them. He would take them in out of spite to hurt you." Every inch of me craves Tyson. God, how I wish we were a normal couple going through a happy time in our lives adopting these boys. The hypocrisy of the man my father is strikes me dumb right here and now. Tyson's words slice through me once again. I can pretend all over again. Demonstrate that I'm truly their daughter.

"I wouldn't call this a fight. It's a discussion. A civilized conversation. One that needed to be hashed out," he informs.

Finally, he moves from his dominating stance by the door to sit next to me. He doesn't bring me in his arms or cocoon me the way he did the other night. I feel the heat from his body, though. It seeps into my pores. It was always that way when we were close to each other. As if we sponged off of one another to stay warm. Both of us hating to go back to our cold, gloomy homes when all we wanted to do was cling to each other. He doesn't need to coddle me over this. In my own weaknesses, I've found my strength. I'm capable of doing it all if I put my mind to it. I've shown it before, and I can attest to it.

"You're right. About all of it. They've taught me many things. All of them I ignored at the time. I don't need anyone to fight my battles for me. This is something I can do on my own."

"You can. But you're not going to. I learned something over the years, Lynne. I know what family means. My friends are my family. I've walked through hell with them. Seen and done shit that would make the devil cringe. Don't expect any of us to stand back and watch you do this alone. We don't work that way. We stick together and fuck shit up. We have luck on our side this time. Did you know Jude's in the process of adopting Theo? He was a foster kid."

"Really? I didn't. I never gave it much thought except to think he had him young. Do you think he'll help me?" I replace my repulsiveness for my father with a laugh. Just discussing this with Tyson makes my heart feel lighter, my poison-filled brain flushing the last remaining bits and pieces out of my system.

"I know he fucking will," he bites out as if I've asked him the dumbest question he's ever heard.

"We'll talk to him about it. By the way, Vivian and Cora stopped by the other day to apologize for their behavior toward me. I told them how happy it made me to see how much they cared about you. I agree with you about family. I feel the same way about Maggie. She knows everything. Do your friends know about the boys?" I ask courageously. My head is spinning crazily with all of this heartfelt news.

"Yes. I had Jude dig around, then another one of my friends, Dane, broke into your father's office to see if he could find proof. It's all in the file. The guys have our back, Lynne. I promise you they do."

"I suppose this is one of those you-have-my-back-and-I-have-yours type of things. Thank you. This isn't going to be easy. I need a lawyer," I say with a slight smile and a delicate edge to my voice.

"No, it isn't. You're not alone, though, remember that. I've got a lawyer. He'll be more than happy to help you." I sigh, lean into his warm body, and welcome the strange feeling of not being alone. It's one of the greatest feelings in the world. That, plus being in his arms.

"Just so you know, I didn't ask Cora and Vivian to come see you; they did that all on their own."

CHAPTER ELEVEN

TYSON

"You good with this?" I ask, close her door, and join her on the deck. I look over at the stunning woman gazing down the beach where my entire clan is sitting around a fire three hours after our talk, where her words, her fight, and her struggles hypnotized me into a deep trance I might never come out of.

Plus, my cock turned instantly hard when she prowled out of her kitchen with a jar of cherries in her hand, her mouth twisted up in a devious smirk. I used to jack off like crazy to images of her mouth moving back and forth, her cheeks hollowing in, knowing her tongue was wrapping around that tiny little stem. I have no clue how she does it, but I'll be damned if it isn't one of the sexiest things I have watched her do. It turned me on back then, and it turns me on even more now.

"I would love nothing more than to meet all of your family and friends," she responds so quickly I do a double take to make sure she isn't doing this for me.

"Don't do this for me, Lynne. Do it for yourself."

"I'm doing it for both of us." She smiles wide. I can't begin to explain how it feels to see an older yet better version of the same one I've missed smearing across her face. It shows me yet again the bravery that shocks my system stumbling in her direction.

We've done more than weave our way through the drudges of hell that have taken over our lives all this time. We're plowing them down, scraping the surface. Extinguishing them one by one until we get to the center of the fire. The giant monstrosity of vindictiveness I'm going to watch burn.

"I'm going to be fighting on his turf, Tyson. I told you when we were eating dinner I'm going to go through with this and I'm going to call the lawyer you told me about. No matter what anyone tries to tell me, those boys mean everything to me and I can't stand by and watch them be raised by someone else any longer when it's my chance to be a mother or a sister, whichever direction I decide to go. I love them enough to start this process before he has a chance to know what's coming at him. I want it to knock him down, to tear him up, and for him to see that he can no longer control me. Mostly, I don't want him anywhere near them." I have nothing. No words of encouragement to throw back at her. She's said it all. And that right there is my biggest fucking problem with all of this. It doesn't have a damn thing to do with her wanting those kids. It's because legally, I won't be a part of it. *They won't be mine.*

They'll be hers and not mine, and every cell in body is trying to understand why fate chose to take her from me, then years later, the boomerang comes flying back landing at my feet where it belongs and I'm not allowed to pick it up and claim it. I should be fighting this fight with her, holding her hand, doing all of this together. Which, in a sense I am. It's just not the way it should be. And quite frankly, it pisses me the fuck right off.

"I say we have a weekend with no stress. You ignore your phone, pack a bag, and help me furnish my apartment." This is the only thing I can think of to get her the weekend that is essential for her. She needs to focus on something else. To break herself free before her cage is rattled beyond either one of our comprehensions. This is not going to be easy.

We talked a little more about her mother stopping by. How she demanded things out of her and how she stood up for herself and Maggie. How the tyrant tried to snag her into admitting what she has on them. Lynne told her off, got right up in her face to tell her never to come back.

We both know that enraged Ellen. She'll take it as a challenge. To push Lynne to her limit. Only we are going to stand back and watch them deteriorate. Hang themselves with the noose that's being custom made for them.

If her mother went flying home on her broomstick to bitch about Lynne flipping her shit, then I have no doubt that fucker will be on his way here the first chance he gets. There's not a chance in hell he will show up on my turf. God help the arrogant motherfucker if he does. He's all kinds of crazy to think about showing up here. The guys will fuck him up if they catch wind of it. So will I.

"I would love that, Tyson," she admits, voice gliding to a stop and her luminous eyes filling to the brim with tears. I'm all man. But one thing I've always hated was being the root to her crying. Good tears or not, they undo me, only proving more that I'm human.

"Come over here, Lynne." I point to the spot right in front of me. I need to touch her.

"Okay, but don't you dare baby me. These are good tears. Happy. Carefree. And I'm not allowing you to take them away from me," Lynne fires back with a cunning smile that nearly trips my feet from under me. Her hair flies all around her pretty little head. Dressed down in a pair of jeans, a hooded sweatshirt with the neck ripped down the middle, and barefoot. Gorgeous. Stunning.

"I would never take anything away from you. I'm going to kiss you. Now, come here," I demand. Her tiny little feet shuffle forward, her tears dry up in an instant, and her smile turns daring, devious, and dangerous. I'm balls deep in, and I haven't even fucked her. But it's coming. It's going to happen, and I'm going to show her what babying her, taking care of her, and what keeping that smile really means to both her and me.

"Not going to keep my hands to myself anymore. If you're coming over to my place where I can take your mind away from all of this, you better be prepared to sleep in my bed. With me."

"Okay," she whimpers. After all this time, whenever she's this close to me, my body reacts the same. My heart leaps and the majority of my blood shoots straight to my dick. Fuck, I'm so tied up over her it's dangerous. She has always twirled me around. Knotted me up in the same way she works the stem from a cherry. Unbelievable. This woman is really here. With me. And she smells so tempting I really hate to share her beauty with everyone tonight. I care about my friends too much to deny them this time to get to know her and for her to know them.

"Fuck, I've missed you so much." My pulse spikes at the same time my mouth meets hers. Lynne presses her hands to my chest; my cock swells and I'll be damned to hell if right here, right now with her teeth biting my lip, her tongue finding its way in my mouth, that I do not see fate for what she's done here. Fate is a fickle little bitch. Her reasoning to everything is her own. She does shit in her time and says the hell with what you want or need or even desire. This is my world, my way, and right now, you had to suffer in order to save two little boys. Deal with it, because look where you are now. Kissing the woman who owns your soul.

"This kiss isn't yours to command, babe. It's mine," I groan into her mouth. Grab her by the waist and hoist her on top of the railing.

"Oh, God," she moans when I tilt her body back, cage her in with a hand to her back, and dart my tongue out to lick up the torn seam of her sweatshirt exposing her chest. I'm under control enough to not become carried away. I just need a taste. One to pacify me until we get to my place, where we can go from there. I don't give a rat's ass if all I do is hold her in my arms all night. The mere idea of falling asleep with her curled into my side is the only thing I care about. *Bull fucking shit. You want her more than you ever have before.* Isn't that the truth. She's all I can think about.

"You are the best person to walk into my life. I'm never letting you go." I grit out the words I wanted to say after the minister pronounced us man and wife. I shove the tainted reminder that she isn't my wife out to the deep roaring sea behind us. Fucking fate can kiss my bare ass. Keel over dead for all I care. Someday, she will be, and everything, everyone who has roadblocked us will rot in hell.

Lynne bites her lip. Our eyes lock in a stare that reduces my manhood to nothing. Absolute stillness surrounds us. Even our heavy breathing ceases to be heard.

"I won't let you go, either. As long as we're by each other's side, the rest of the world can all go fuck themselves," she promises. I see it in the depths of her green eyes, the deepest part of her lenses, and it flashes so brightly it's damn near blinding.

"Christ, Lynne. Our minds think so much alike," I call out. My mouth resumes it's provincial taking. I consume her mouth in a kiss that grabs me out of years of depression over this woman. An assurance of a future that will take the time to get where we want. I can already see the flag waving far off in the distance.

We engage each other's mouths. A no-tongues banded combat of sexual suggestions. I need to stop this before we get too carried away. I'm a man who hasn't been inside the woman with the only face I've wanted to stare down at. The only woman who has been able to see me for who I am. Ending it with one long, soulful sweep of my tongue across hers, I pull away. Lean my forehead against hers and catch my breath as I inhale her scent.

"Let me take you to meet everyone," I whisper, my blood pressure going down, my heart reverting to its steady beat. She lowers herself down, grabs my hand, and carelessly starts tugging me down the beach to where everyone is hanging out.

"My family can try all they want to come between us this time. It won't happen. I've always belonged to you and you to me. And those boys, they belong to me, too," she says, slows her pace, and links her arm through mine. Her head held high. Brave. Always so Goddamn brave.

This is all about her. An unselfish woman who is going to be a great mother. My needs don't play a part in this equation right now. They'll come. After I make sure hers are met. She's chosen to face her biggest fear. To shut him down and conquer that shit. I've never been more proud of her than I am at this very moment. She blows me away.

She admitted at dinner that she knew. All this fucking time she's been seeing those boys as often as she can. Pretending to be an old family friend of their mother's. Christ, I'm so fascinated and fired up by this woman on my arm that if hell froze over right now, I'd be the one to melt it down. For her.

I feel like fucking exploding with the way she's waltzed back into my life. Stormed her way through my darks clouds to make me see the light.

"I'm going to tell Jacob and Joshua about you the next time I see them," she whispers with so much anxiousness behind it that a sense of relief washes over me. I'm not sure what replaces it. Possibly a tad bit of fear of my own. The probability that those boys may not like me.

"I will meet them on your terms."

"Meet who?" Riddick perches up from his chair. Eyes are darting with a subtle gleam from me to Lynne.

"Meet all of you. Hi, I'm Lynne." She sticks out her hand for him to take. I nearly laugh when Riddick looks down at her hand, shakes his head, and tucks her to his chest, bends and whispers something into her ear, causing her to nod. Fucker thinks he's sneaky. I find myself standing there invisible while she wanders around introducing herself to everyone. Laughing. Freely. Christ. Beauty. Only a sick son of a bitch would want to take that away from her.

"I've heard good things about you, Doctor Chapman." Sylvia Shepard straightens her spine, approaches, and shakes Lynne's hand. And, for the time being, I've lost her as she greets both Sylvia and Ron. The three of them engaging in talk that makes her body relax.

"You still have your balls, or does she own them now?" I scoff as I try to keep my voice light to answer Jude's dumb-ass question. She's always owned them. I'm not admitting it to this smart-ass fucker, though. Don't matter if he can see it or not.

"Last time I checked, they were still attached to my dick." Lynne glances over her shoulder to seek me out. Eyes are twinkling from the flames. Fuck. I'm a liar. "I'm a better man because of her. Not afraid to admit it. Same as you, same as Riddick." Another layer of thin ice cleared. We're thawing more with every passing second.

"There isn't a damn thing wrong with confessing our love. If any man thinks there is, then he isn't a man at all. I'm happy for you, brother. You took a giant leap forward. Don't ever let it go. Life doesn't get any better than falling for a woman who loves you back."

"Isn't that the truth," I answer as I stand there like a fucking fool with my eyes glued to the back of Lynne's head. Not quite sure if what I'm feeling for her is what one would call love quite yet. At least not what he has with Vivian. It's something, though. A beginning to what no doubt will be a happy ending. I'm an even bigger fool if I stand here any longer and try to convince myself that I don't love her. It's impossible not to. The woman has strung me up and wrung me out already.

"I do love her. I've never stopped. It'll take some time to get back to where we belong. That's the main reason why the shit going down with her father needs to come to an end before he takes something else away from her. Something she may not come back from." A knot bobs up and down freely in my throat. Yo-yoing its nasty, bitter taste to the surface.

"You both appear to be in a good place, my friend. I don't want to spoil it. We need to talk. I filled these guys in about our visit to Richard. Does she know everything?" I grab the neck of the beer from Dane's outstretched hand, shoot him a cautionary glance when I notice Vivian and Cora heading our way.

"She knows. Got a lot of shit to tell you guys, just not around her or them. She wants to get to know all of you. Give her this. Not for me but for her. For you." I don't have to stand here and peddle shit in their direction. Her past is forgotten. Forgiven. We've buried it. It's time to breathe. Time to live. And this right here is perfect for her. Lynne and I, we come from totally different backgrounds, yet we've never had a real family, not together anyway. She needs them as much as I do. Possibly more.

"You mind telling me what you whispered in her ear?" I implore. Riddick pulls his cigar out of his mouth, spits the end into the sand, and flashes me a half-cocked smile.

"Welcomed her to the family, man." He shrugs as if what he, what all of them belted out of their mouths was no big deal. It's every damn thing to me. Soon it will be to her, too.

I stare at them all for a few moments before tipping my beer back and topping it off with a grin. I'm not used to freely opening up about my feelings. They've been closed off for so long; it's foreign as fuck to stand out here amongst all of them discussing my intimate state of mind I've kept hidden.

"I'll be back in a few minutes," Lynne hollers over the roar of the fire, the crashing of the waves, and the laughter from the boys tossing a ball in the dark. I'm not sure why but noticing the way she's looking at me, the smile on her face she's desperately trying to hide, makes me wink like a high school kid trying to flirt with the girl who shyly keeps looking at him. Fuck. I want her. Badly. Desperately.

I lift my chin just as she turns and walks with Cora, Vivian, and their mother up toward their house. My eyes trained to the sway of her ass.

I battle the urge to go grab her. To kiss her, claim her right here in front of my family. To scream that this woman who used to drive me crazy with her lack of confidence around other girls who came from nothing would see her as the rich kid who felt sorry for them. They weren't insecurities at all, because they were drilled in her head that it was improper for her to want to hang out with them for the simple fact she came from money and they did not; or it was uncalled for when she went out of her way to help the not-so fortunate kids at school who couldn't grasp their assignments. She defied her parents at every corner. Came to me when life became too much for her to handle. And now she's walking away with two of the strongest women I know. Her hands flowing strong by her sides instead of stuffed in the pocket of her hoodie like she used to do. A hoodie her mom would fall over dead if she saw her wearing.

I don't care what she says or how she's been convinced she isn't strong enough to accomplish anything on her own. She's a role model for strength. The truest definition of it.

"She'll be fine." Riddick breaks my train of thought just as Ron saunters up to us, cooler in hand and a loose smirk on his face.

"I know," I say, finish off my beer, toss it on the ground, and pull another out of the cooler.

"They went to show her their homes. Suppose they'll be a while. I'm happy for you, Tyson. The guys here filled me in. I want you to know I'll do everything I can to help." Jesus. Fuck. I need to get my emotions in check before I drop to my Goddamn knees over the welcome these people have for her.

"I appreciate the offer. The less you become involved, the better it will make me feel. We're dealing with a man who doesn't give a fuck about his own children, Ron."

"All the more reason for me to be involved," he replies as if Lynne is already in his veins the same way she's embedded in mine.

"Son of a bitch. There you guys are." We all snap our heads up at the sound of Dominic's voice. His long strides are picking up pace. My hand grips the neck of the bottle the closer he gets. Something isn't right.

"What's going on?" Dane asks. The evening air begins filling up with everyone's stiffness. I know what the fuck is going on. Dominic has been keeping an eye on Richard. The bastard is on his way here. He doesn't give a flying fuck if it's late at night. Her father is coming after her. That asshole is avoiding my warning. I've spent my entire adult life reading people. Interrogating them until they cave. It's written all over Dominic, and I am pissed. I should have known that prick wouldn't wait to see if I followed through with my threat to expose him. Lynne was so right about his life being a movie. It wouldn't surprise me one bit if the idiot doesn't edit it into a documentary about how men are differentiated in a world full of powerful women. He is a stupid fuck.

"How far away is he?" I choke out, my mind already reeling with anger. With all that is holy, I wish to hell I could stand here and greet that sorry excuse for a parent kindly. Instead, I'm praying to God to control my anger and not allow me to blow his fucking head clear off his shoulders and shove it up his ass.

Jude is right about my balls disappearing. It's only been a matter of days since Lynne and I have tried to work shit out. To be honest, she's had a hold of them since the day I met her; it's only taken me this long to feel the squeeze, the tight grip, and the warm sensation in my gut that the years we've lost don't mean a thing when you honest to God never stopped loving someone. I fucking love her. I need to protect her. This is why my feet are moving toward the house. I need to get her out of here, but I'll be damned to hell once again. It's too late.

CHAPTER TWELVE

LYNNE

"We need to stop the rotten motherfucker." My body stiffens at hearing the voice coming from below.

"That's Tyson," I yell nervously, never taking my eyes off Cora as we all peer over the edge of the rooftop. My heart instantly drops to the ground when I notice him dash in between the two houses with the rest of the guys right behind him.

There's only one I person I can think of who would have Tyson acting out the way he is.

My father. He's here.

I should have asked Tyson to whisk me away to his apartment instead of allowing my hopes to take over. That for once in my life my family would leave me the hell alone. But no. Here he is, barreling down my street as if he owns me. The devil has come to town.

For the life of me, I will never understand what I've done to deserve this. *Evil.* The whole lot of them. *Why do they hate me so much?*

"Get in the house," Riddick yells at the boys who look scared to death. One can only pray that my father isn't here on some instantaneous mission to ruin my hopes and dreams once again.

"Fat chance, Lynne," I mumble to myself.

The world can swallow me whole any time it wants. This is embarrassing.

I wait until I'm certain Ron and Dominic have the boys secured in the house. My body is coming alive with fury. Pins and needles are pricking away at my gut to get down there and make that man see I'm not going to be pushed around anymore.

"What on earth is going on?" Sylvia's voice is full of panic. God, how I wish I grew up with parents who loved the way she and Ron do. A few minutes in their company was all it took for me to realize they love hard and deep.

I haven't felt this comfortable with people I barely know in my entire life. Except for Maggie. They are all laid-back. So full of joy it was beginning to make my heart sing to a happy, joyful beat.

"It's my father. He's here." My voice trembles, but I stay strong. I want these women to like me for who I am. Not out of pity for what they might witness or sympathy for what I've lost. For me. A woman who is capable of standing on her own two feet. Facing the corrupted values of a hateful man head-on. That's all I've ever wanted was to be accepted for being human. For making mistakes that I've owned up to.

I want to curl up in the corner and bury my head in my hands. These women opened their minds and hearts to me as if we've all been friends our entire lives, and now this? A half hour or so was all I'm being given to the start of what assuredly was becoming one of the best nights I've had in years. Tyson and I had a wonderful discussion about the boys at dinner. The kiss he claimed was his. The way he looked at me the way he always does. I matter to him. He matters to me. I'm over this infatuation my blood family has to destroy me. I've been pushed too far now. It's time to dig my claws in and scar them the way they've done me.

Tyson left me in knots. Wanting, craving all of him, and now I'm being sucked back to a hell I've been dying to escape from.

My chest tightens.

"Please stay here." I swallow hard. My lead-filled bare feet leading me to the stairs. The smile that brightened all our faces moments ago fading away. Slipping out to sea in the dead of night.

I'm going to kill him with my bare hands.

All they have done is carve out holes inside of me. Plugged them with their lies. I am so sick and tired of being their victim. I want to live happily, damn it. To be a free spirit with my little brothers by my side. I won't allow him to take them away from me. And that is exactly why he's here. Instead of being a man and openly admitting they are his children, he's come here to find out what I know and to try and convince me to shut my mouth.

My feet hit the pavement just as the loud echo coming from Tyson's voice stings my ears. I run down the little driveway, hammering the short distance to my house.

"This is private property, Richard. Get the hell out of here. I told you. Do not fuck with me. Either you climb back in your car and leave, or so help me God, I'll cuff you, toss you in jail, and forget you are there." My father smiles. His gray hair slicked back, his suit pristine as he stands with his car door wide open. His arms crossed over his chest. He's acting calm when he's anything but. I can see the steam bleeding out of his ears. He wasn't expecting a welcome wagon full of men who hate him to be here. Arrogant prick.

If I didn't want to battle this on my terms, I would stand here and let them take turns beating him to his death.

"Last I checked, my daughter owned this house." He slams the door, and I let out a strangled cry. My body is no longer concealed in darkness.

My father drops his gaze, cranks his head, and a pair of dark, intense eyes cast my way. Their spell is quite demanding. Intimidating. And yet I stand tall, edging my way closer to be seen. I want him to see me. All of me. No longer hidden shadows.

"Last time I checked, I thought I told your wife to give you a message. I do own this house. This is my property, and I do not want you here. Leave." Tyson starts to move toward me. I halt him with my hand.

"No. I can handle this. Please. All of you stay back," I tell him steadily. "It's been a long time coming, Tyson. He needs to hear me this time."

So much has changed in a matter of days. My strength to stand up for myself is one of them. I'm at the top of my game now. He's dead to me.

"My wife is your mother. She is why I'm here. We are worried about you."

I laugh. It sounds deranged, just like him. "She is not my mother.

Not anymore. If she were any kind of mother to me, we wouldn't be standing here having this discussion. If either one of you had been a parent to me, I wouldn't hate you. And believe me, I do hate you. My entire life you have taken from me. Not once have you given me what a parent should give their children." I hope he smells the revulsion I feel for him. He blanches. Good. I hope my cuts turn fatally infectious.

Those deep, seedy eyes of his reach inside of me to see if I'm not only speaking about myself but those boys, too. I give nothing away. He hasn't brought them up, yet, and I'll be damned if I will, either. If he does, he better be prepared for his Lifetime movie to change directions and become an HBO original series, because I'll turn it into one and he'll be the victim who ends up dying in the end. Death by a daughter.

I'm not scared of what my father can do to me anymore. I'm numb to it. None of that means a damn thing when he can step up and pull two more things out from under me.

What if he does? No. I refuse to think it. He will never take them away from me. I simply won't allow it.

"Are you listening to yourself? This has gone on long enough. I allowed you to buy this house. Become a doctor. And this is how you repay me? We need to talk. I won't discuss your irrational behavior anymore in front of them." He didn't allow me to do anything. I chose on my own. What the hell?

My regard easily trains itself in the direction of four men standing in a row. All of them have their fists clenched. Three of them are staring wildly at my father, while the one who owns my heart is looking at me with more affection than he ever has before. I want to run to him. Hide in the security of his big strong arms. I can't. Not until I lay this day to rest. Get him gone and forget he was ever here.

"I believe you have the wrong definition of me. This is me being sensible. I didn't ask your permission to buy this house. I did it on my own. As far as school goes, I used you to get what I wanted. Now I'm done. I want you to stay out of my life forever. You came here demanding something of me instead of asking. Just like she did today. Not once in my life have you ever asked me what I wanted. It's always what *you* want. What *your wife* wants. What *my sisters* want. I'm not going anywhere with you. You are not welcome in my house. You are nothing to me. *Nothing.* My love died for you the day you deceived me into losing the only man I've loved. So, as far as I'm concerned, I am not your daughter. You have one minute to get off my property, or I'll let them arrest you." I catch my breath. My chest heaves to the point it burns from spitting out words I've wanted to say for so long.

"My wife is your mother, Lynne. I believe she told you that will never change. He's tainting you against us, don't you see that? Whatever he tells you isn't true. I'm your father. I do love you. How can you not see that all I've ever wanted was the best for you? I'm trying to protect you. He's not it, Lynne. He's not." He draws out his bullshitting love for me a little late in my life. The same as his wife did.

My soul rips in half. It quivers when one piece detaches itself and shatters while the other half remains intact. He's never loved me a day in my life. Lying piece of shit.

"Protect me? You broke me. You and her. I was in love with him. I still am. A parent should protect their child in every way. That includes their heart. Not destroy it. You people are certifiably crazy. I have openings if you need help." Oh, God, my anger is getting the best of me. I feel horrible for saying that. Just because I care about the few patients I've been blessed with. They aren't crazy because they need guidance. But this man is. He should be locked up because of his actions. No treatment. No shoulder to lean on and definitely no one who cares.

"Christ, Lynne. Look at him. He's nobody. A fucking bastard." I want to throw up all over him for speaking about Tyson this way.

"Watch it, motherfucker," Riddick implies. Dear ole dad completely ignores him. At this moment, I wish he would do something to get arrested. Step across the line of the law that he's been teetering on for years. I would love nothing more than to see it all be slammed in his face.

"I am looking at him. He's all I see. He's a saint. A man who forgave me. You do not get to come here and call him names, especially one that is reserved for you. He has a name. A name that should have been mine. You ripped my life from me. Stole it right from under me. How many times do I have to tell you people this? I was out of my mind sick with cancer. I could have been diagnosed terminally, and you still would have made me believe he was going to leave me. Or worse, turn into a man like you." I've wasted enough of my day on the likes of these dysfunctional people. I want my carefree weekend, and he's trying to ruin it.

"That's enough. You're done talking to her. Come here, Lynne, please?" I walk in Tyson's direction willingly. Grounded. Relieved for once that I have my feet planted firmly in spite of people trying to knock me down. Even though this is the beginning of a feud I may not win, I feel better for standing up to a man who has always wanted to hurt me.

His arms wrap around me, pulling me in for a hug. God, I feel relieved. The air around me clear.

"You'll pay for this, you little bitch. This is your last warning, Lynne. All of you." Tyson's arm stiffens. Every muscle in his body goes tight. Flexing up against me.

"What did you call her?" I've never seen Tyson so angry, and I've never been lifted off the ground as quickly as I am now. Plunked on my feet in front of Jude as I watch in utter horror as Tyson somehow leaps off the cement and slams my father to the hood of his car. My heart jumps in my throat.

"I fucking warned you," Tyson growls. He is furious. His arm slings across my father's neck, pinning him down in a deathly hold. I want to scream for Tyson to choke him.

"Tyson. He's not worth it." This is surprisingly coming from Riddick.

"Don't fucking 'Tyson' me. This scum needs to mind his own business. He needs to apologize for calling her a name, and he needs to be taught a lesson for every wrongdoing he has committed."

"Fuck you and her," my father spits.

"What in the hell is going on out here?" Jude pulls me into him, while I crane my neck to the wired hum of Maggie.

"Maggie, put that gun down!" Riddick yells from his spot next to me. Shivers slide across my skin. Restriction holds the tightness in my throat. I can't breathe.

"I will do no such thing, Riddick. Not when I peek out my window after hearing loud voices and this piece of trash calling Lynne a bitch.

Now, you listen to me, buddy. If you ever come down my street again and threaten my girl here, I won't hesitate to shoot you for crossing onto private property. We do not want you here. Get in your car and go. And don't even think about taking this out on Lynne. I'll chew you up and choke on you before I let you drag her down again. Now, get." Oh. My. God. No woman in my life has ever stood up for me the way she is before. I'm not sure if I want to laugh at the scene playing out in front of me or cry.

"You heard her. Go." Tyson releases his hold, backs up, and my father straightens himself out, yanks his door open, and climbs in his car. The purr of his engine calms me.

He backs up slowly while never taking his eyes away from mine. They are giving me a message. A dangerous one. He's telling me I've made a choice, one he will never agree with. The one I'll regret. For all of us to watch our backs. It's a bad thing for him that we will be watching out for one another. There's no escaping what went down here tonight. How these men and Maggie had my back the entire time.

"Dad." Oh, no. It's Theo. My shoulders sag from the worry in this young man's voice.

This is an awful situation for a teenager to witness.

"I'm terribly sorry," I sob.

Jude releases his hold on me. My legs want to give out. "Everything is alright, son." Jude slights himself to acknowledge Theo. Then he spins me around to face him. "Not sure why you're sorry when it's obvious you're a fighting warrior. And don't ever apologize to us again. We protect what's ours, and you are part of us; you need to catch onto that quick. Now, go get your man, Lynne."

I'm struggling to breathe, and it has nothing to do with my father coming here. It has everything to do with that innocent young man witnessing something he should never see. It has to do with them all being here to stand by me while all I've done since the day I moved here was cause them grief, and yet they're still here. Still telling me I'm a part of them.

My legs finally give out just as the little bit of air in my lungs escapes with a whoosh that fires up my chest. I expect to crack my knees on the cement. I don't. I'm caught, lifted into the air, and inhale a scent that's becoming intoxicatingly familiar.

"Make sure Maggie's gun is registered. I got this from here," Tyson instructs, while my mind whirls into a stammering mess.

"Maggie. We have to make sure she's protected," I sputter out, my voice on the verge of breaking. I'm fighting hard not to cry or to admit how much it all hurts. The name my own father called me. The way he looked right through me as if I truly didn't exist.

"She'll be fine. Everyone will be. You can talk to her on Monday," he affirms, hoists me into his truck, tucks my hair behind my ear, and lifts my chin. Sweetly, his thumb strokes back and forth across flesh that melts like warm, rich syrup. Tyson is searching to make sure I'm alright. And I am. I may be shaken up, stinging in places I've been stung before. But I'm over the past that's been haunting my future. It's time to force my hand. To continue to show them what I'm truly made of. Strength. Power and determination to bring them down.

"I'm good. I'll be better if you'll get me out of here." I love my home. The serenity the beach brings. The tranquility of the sea. I was promised a weekend away. Whether it be across town at his place or a run-down motel, I do not care, as long as I'm spending it with him.

"Tell me where your keys are." I briefly glance away from him, my eyes landing on Jude, who has both of his hands on Theo's shoulders. Speaking in a hushed tone. They look so comfortable together. A father who's consoling his child. I want that so, so, much. Not only for me but for Tyson, too. For us to teach, to learn, to love.

"On the kitchen counter," I exhale, my vision turning back to him. Soft eyes, a twitch of his lips. A half-ass smile.

"Wha—?" I'm not allowed to finish. Hands fist my hair. His mouth lands on mine, and it's violently brutal. Deliriously sweet. It creates peace in my spirit. Air in my lungs, possibilities of everything unattainable that's been far from my reach.

I've never wanted a man to touch me the way I want him in all of my life. It's agony waiting this out. Humiliating that I should have to.

I exhale. He inhales. Our breathing becomes one, and I'm dying a little. Tiny little breaths escape my lungs. Bubbles form in my lower abs, popping. Producing more with every hot-blooded touch. I'm a grown woman being devoured by a man I never thought would touch me again. And I want him inside of me. To hunt me, string me up, and turn me inside out.

"You exposed who you really are tonight. I'm so fucking proud of you for standing up for yourself, Lynne. You are so brave. Don't move." He presses his words against my lips. Oh, God. It's amazing how a few words from the right person can lift a broken soul and put it back together again. That you step backward one small step at a time before you take the final step forward to drop away. Vanish. To freefall from every mistake you have made in your life. I feel so adored that it shakes me up. An exceptional touch of devotion.

"Tyson."

"Fuck, you are so damn beautiful. I can't tear my eyes away from you. Your beauty doesn't have a thing to do with what happened here. It shines all around you, sweetheart. You are so good. So full of love that it angers me to no end that man is unseeing to the beauty he created." Oh, fuck. Gone is the angry Tyson, replaced with a sweet, devoted man. I love him. I want him. And I'm going to have him.

"I'm forgetting he was here. I don't need them to show me what being wanted is. I want you, Tyson. All of you," I find myself saying. I mean every word of it.

"God, Lynne. I want you so bad my body is taking pleasure from hurting. I need to feel you, to taste, touch, and hold you. I'll be right back." He kisses me briefly before turning away.

I wouldn't think of moving after that.

He wants me in the same way I want him. My body shakes as my mind holds itself hostage in a faraway trance. Hands, lips, legs tangled together. Clothes being torn off. Exploring one another for the first time in years.

A forgotten ache forms between my legs. One that has been hidden away since the last time we were together. It crawls up my spine. Bumps up my skin and develops a warmth through my veins, my cells, and centers somewhere in between. It pounds my heart, my ears, and my existence to tell me this is all real. He's here. He's mine and I will never let him go.

It brings me joy to watch him jog up to Jude and Theo, pat them both on the back before disappearing around the corner of my house.

I close my eyes, tilt my head back, and store away every sour thought from today. All I can see now are my little boys. The ones who adore me as much as I do them. They'll love Tyson. I know they will.

CHAPTER THIRTEEN

TYSON

"You get her father out of your head." Jude snakes his perceptive eyes at me. God willing this man knows me fucking well.

"Already forgotten. You good, Theo?" His eyes shift from his dad to me, where they lock down tight. Pisses me off he had to witness this. The kid has been through enough in his life, and to see this kind of behavior from a grown man, well, fuck. I don't know what to think. Except the kid is damn lucky to have Jude.

"I'm good. Sure wish I could have right-hooked the piece of shit and knocked him on his ass." His comeback has both me and Jude chuckling.

"Theo was bred to be yours."

"I couldn't agree with you more," Jude states proudly.

"If there is a next time, he's all yours, buddy." I turn from Theo to Jude, lowering my voice, so Lynne doesn't hear me.

"Richard's hiding something else. On Monday, we start digging deeper. I'll talk to Sarge. Fill him in on everything. Richard is pretending to care way too much for my liking; he came here to not only try and squash me but to see if she knows about those kids. There's more to this than he's letting on."

I squeeze both their shoulders, jog into the house, swipe her keys and the bag she packed, and lock up. My heart swells when I round the corner to see the two of them still standing there talking.

Theo is listening to every word Jude is telling him. Respectfully.

Prime example how showing your kid that they mean everything to you right there. Making sure they are nothing but okay. That what went down here was all kinds of wrong and Lynne deserved none of it.

Riddick and Dane must have taken right off to check on everyone else.

Richard had me enraged with anger. I could feel it hovering on the edge of ballistic. It all ended when Lynne showed up and told him off, only to start back up again when he called her a bitch. He can call me whatever the fuck he wants, but when you disrespect a woman and do it in front of others, that shit will never sit well with me. Especially when it comes to her.

I refrained from killing him. Knew it right down to the soles of my feet that she could handle herself. And she did. More than I ever thought possible. She didn't allow him to roll her around in the dirt anymore. But I had enough. It took every bit of restraint I had not to coldcock him straight to the gates of hell. All I can say for now is, he's a lucky bastard for Maggie showing up the way she did, or I may be sitting in a jail cell calling Thomas Holder for my needs of his services instead of Lynne's.

My gait doubles its strides to my truck. Damn, I could stand here and watch her the rest of the night. She deserves all the good out of life, and I'll be the bastard he called me to make sure she gets it. "You ready?" Her eyes are closed, head tilted back, exposing a neck that I want to lick, suck, and run my tongue over. Beauty. Every glamorous inch of her. Inside and out.

"I changed my mind." For one brief second my heart drops. Chains rattle loud. Caging me in a battle of confusion.

Until the next words out of her mouth lift it right back where it belongs. "This is my house; he's not going to drive me away from here. We can shop tomorrow if you want, but tonight I want to stay here." Fuck me. Strong. Smart. And so damn beautiful. Gazing over at me as if she can see right through me. And I'd let her if I could. I have nothing to hide. Not from her.

"Get out of the truck," I demand. Roughly. Her eyes pop. Electrical energy jolts between us and my dick jerks from the heat blazing off her. "Now." No more fucking around. I really don't care where we are as long as she's with me. Hell, I had already told myself there was no way in hell I was leaving her by herself at night, so fuck buying me shit that eventually I may not need. It's fast, impulsive, and way early in our relationship to be thinking this way, but I don't give a shit about that, either.

She gets out of the truck; I grab her hand and pull her alongside me. Running up the steps to her porch and placing her in front of me.

The only thing I care about right now is seeing her come undone. I need her with her ass in my hands and her legs wrapped around my waist. Her mouth on mine and her taste on my tongue.

I reach around her to unlock her door. Her breath hitches and I swear to God I can hear her heart pounding in a rapid frenzy inside of her chest when I press my front up against her back. Lynne knows just as well as I do that the instant she pushes her way through this door, there's no going back for us. The hurt we've both bled out remains outside of this home. It's me and her together.

It doesn't matter where we are, where we've been. It's forever with her.

"I'm all in," I express when she pauses in the kitchen, flicks on a light, and stops in her tracks, her back to me. And again, my heart sinks wondering what's going through her head right now. I would never push her into doing something she isn't ready for. She's been pushed enough.

"Me too. If we are going to be doing this, all of this, I don't want you to treat me as if I'm breakable, Tyson. I want every part of you." She turns to face me. The lightest of green pools trail up my body. By the time they reach my face, they are dark. Forest green. Sinful. Wicked. My feet move across the polished hardwood floor. Her bag lands at my feet with a thud. And fuck all if I can't wait to dirty her up. Bury myself in her sweetness and die a happy Goddamn man.

"You aren't breakable, Lynne. You're irreplaceable." I lift her up by the waist, her long legs wrapping around me, and my mouth hovers over hers.

"You can't say things like that to me and not expect me to melt."

Fuck. I'd like to crack her across her ass and tell her she better get used to hearing me say whatever I want to her. But I don't. She'll get used to it. "Is your bedroom upstairs?" I march down the hall, my hands squeezing her ass until she gasps.

"Yes," she answers.

"Shit. I can't wait to have you."

It's fucking dark in here, and yet I manage to climb two steps at a time without tumbling over, shoving her pants down, and taking her on these stairs. I reach the top, twist us to the right where a soft glow comes from the end of the hall. I tug her hair back, exposing her neck. It's been taunting me all night.

My tongue darts out to taste.

My mouth takes hold and sucks.

"Goddamn, Lynne." Her moans have me all kinds of screwed up. Whimpers. Sighs. And the heat coming off her breaks me out in a cold, damp sweat.

I'm nervous as hell when I cross the threshold to her room. It all fades away the second I toss her on the bed, her wild mane of hair a mess from the wind. Her eyes are wild and full of passion for me.

"I don't care what anyone says; you were born to be mine the same way I was for you. Christ, you are the most stunning woman I have ever seen." I need her in the same capacity that I need air. To be able to breathe.

She doesn't utter a word. I swallow when she perches up on her elbows, tucks her feet into the bed, and sits straight up. Her pulse quivers in her neck. Tongue darts out of that sexy little mouth. Then my woman's stunning face vanishes for a fraction when she reaches down and pulls her sweatshirt over her head. My dick cries out in agonizing pain when I take in her generous breasts covered by a teal lace bra. Her rose-colored nipples are prominently hard. "Motherfucker. You are far from breakable. You're a powerful woman who's bringing me to my knees." I would drop now if she asked me to.

I can't take not touching her anymore. Caring for Lynne consumes me. It shreds away every bad day I've had for thirteen years. I tug my shirt over my head, bend one knee and then the other until I'm straddling her legs. My hand shakes as I reach out and run a finger across her collarbone. She shivers; bumps form on her silky skin.

"I don't have it in me to be gentle tonight. Don't have condoms either. I need to fuck you. Bare." It's the only way I know how to tell her there isn't anything coming between us again. We aren't kids anymore. I've always been safe. I've never wanted inside of a woman without protection. I do her. It will kill me if she says no. But I care too much about her to not understand. I'll wait.

"I want that more than anything," she whispers. I briefly close my eyes. Thanking God for this caring woman who trusts me. That's all I want to hear.

Reaching around her, I unhook her bra, slide it off her arms, and fill my eyes with her. Her breasts are begging for me as badly as I'm begging for them.

"Lie back," I instruct. She does what she's told. Her chest heaving as her nipples harden more with every breath. I unsnap her jeans, yank them down her legs, her matching panties follow, and a vision I never expected to see again in my life lies before me.

A thin-trimmed patch of hair between her legs, a scar that beckons my tongue rests right above. Perfect. Mine. A treasure.

"I don't know where to start on this canvas of perfection. Here?" I ask, running my finger from her bellybutton to the dent between her tits. My fingers drawing circles across every inch of her upper body, her nipples, down her sides and back again.

"You have no idea how it feels when you touch me." Oh, I certainly do. She's the one who has no idea.

"I know how I feel and I need more than touching," I reply, quirk a brow, dip my head, and take one of her nipples in my mouth. I lose control. Sucking. Biting. Discovering. I grab her other breast, rolling her nipple between my fingers, palming it in my hand while my mouth explores more of her. I trail soft kisses down her stomach. Take hold of both her breasts and squeeze. Her sounds ring out and into my ears.

I want to taste her so fucking bad that I nearly blow.

My tongue paths its way across her scar. Her stomach indents from her harsh intake of breath. I want her to know that even though there's pain behind it, it's part of her. A part as beautiful as her untainted soul.

"Fuck. You smell good. I'm going to drive you crazy. Fuck you until

you beg me to finish. I'll never be finished, not for the rest of my life."
She shudders, and my heart breaks free from the last chain that's held
me hostage. That rusted bitch crashes and turns to copper-colored ash.

"Oh, hell," she moans. Her ass starts squirming, her legs opening in
invitation, and I inhale. Her pretty pussy inches from my face. Control
goes out the Goddamn window. Thank fuck she doesn't want gentle,
because that's one step behind control.

My cock hurts like hell. My spine burns like a bitch. But all I care
about is pleasing her, making her come all over my mouth. Tasting
what's mine. Pushing it into another atmosphere and guiding it home.

Her breath hitches when I slide off the edge of the bed and my hand
dives to the button of my jeans.

"I need these off, because the instant you come in my mouth is all
it's going to take for me to sink inside of you." I tug them off, not once
taking my darkened gaze from hers. Lynne watches me with hooded
eyes. They shift down my chest, across my tattoos, and go wide when
she sees my cock spring free. I toe them off, grip my dick, and stroke.

"Tyson." My name is a prayer answered from her sweet, sweet lips.

"Right here, Lynne. Spread those legs as far as you can." She does
and good Lord Almighty, it's the most perfect thing I've seen in my life.

"Jesus," I spit out. Her pussy is glistening wet; my mouth dries up.
It's parched, pleading to be energized by the beauty before me.

I lean in and swipe my tongue up the middle of her seam. I have
never tasted anything so beneficial to me in my life. Sweet. Satisfying.
Sexy.

It has been too long without her. Longer than any man should have
to wait to give and take what belongs to him.

"Fuck, baby," I mumble against her warm, wet core. I need more. I
skate a finger down the soft row of hair, sinking it right in next to my
tongue. I eat her like a dessert. I finger her like a man gone wild, and
I watch her through the barely open lids of my eyes as she grips the
sheets, her ass lifting in the air, and she comes all over my mouth. It's
all I can take.

I rake my gaze over her body. Leave her sweetness on my chin. Every
inch of her is sheer perfection. From the way her toes dig into the bed

to the way she trembles when I climb on top her and, finally, fucking finally have her under me.

"Hold on to the rails, Lynne," I order, sliding my hands up her sides, palming her breasts one more time, and taking her mouth. Her tongue laps her taste right off me. Teeth start tugging on my bottom lip.

"I missed you," I declare, pressing my chest into hers. A part of me wants to tell her I love her. It's the only part of the conversation she had with her father that sunk to my bones. It belongs here with her and me. A love like ours. Love that lasts. I can't. Not yet. Nonetheless, her telling him has inflated my heart, and I'm leaving it there.

"I missed you, too." Christ, this woman is everything to me.

I grab my cock, close my eyes, and feel her as I begin to climb inside. All of her. Mine. Belongs only to me.

"Tyson," she moans, her body arching upward. Her hands are turning knuckle-white as her arms shake not to let go of the steel frame to her bed.

"I know," I say. Sinking so deep inside of her that I still.

I have never felt anything so good in my life. So right, so perfect that I don't want to move out of fear this won't be real. It is real. It's her. Lynne. The woman who has taken my soul with her everywhere.

"I need you to fuck me, please." Breakable, my Goddamn ass. Satiable. Fuckable. Unforgettable.

"Like this?" I wrap my finger around her ankle and place it on my shoulder. If it's possible, my dick goes deeper. Lynne sucks in a lungful of air, and I fuck her then. My hips are pulling out and thrusting back in. Taking and giving until I can't see straight.

Over and over until sweat forms between her breasts, my hard driving rattling her bed.

I squeeze her nipple, pull it into my mouth, and bite. I feel the gasp she cries out all the way to her pussy, where she clenches around my dick when she starts her spiraling release. Those powerful noises are consuming my mind, and I come with a growl tearing from my spine straight out of the gates of heaven. Our eyes lock. They stay that way for the longest time. Seconds. Minutes. It could be forever for all I care, because I just fucked the only woman I have ever loved.

"Can I touch you now?" She smiles up at me. Drops those dainty little hands and grabs my ass.

"You want more?" I tease.

"You mean more to me than you will ever know," I say then lower my head down to rest on her forehead. I can't move. Not going to either. My cock is half hard still nestled inside of her. Right where it should be.

"I've always wanted you." And there it is. All I've ever craved to hear. Whether it has her pulling me around by my dick or not. I really don't fucking care. One taste of her has awakened what lay paralyzed for years. It's pushing through the sludge. Extending its hand for me to reach out and grab it. Love. A never-ending, soul-stealing kind of love.

CHAPTER FOURTEEN

LYNNE

I see life so openly now. So differently from the way it used to be. I'm anxious to get this started. I'm powerful enough to see this through, and I owe a lot of it to the man by my side, who single-handedly opened my eyes the rest of the way with a single touch of his hand. His sweet, sweet words and the way he holds me at night.

He's a blessing, an inspiration, and I'm so glad he's here.

I spent months lying in bed wondering if I'd fall asleep and not wake up. I'd know nothing of it if I did. There were days when my pain became too much and all I wanted to do was suck myself somewhere deep so I could cope. My body took a beating, my heart had reached the end, and I thrashed in agony with nightmares no human mind should ever dream about.

The constant talks with the nurses, the doctors, the staff telling me I was going to be fine didn't mean a thing to me as I lay there alone night after night wishing someone would hold me. That the splintering words from my parents, the lies my hand wrote on a thin piece of paper didn't pain me as much as the cancer did. Carve a hole in my heart as big as the gloomy, vacant spot inside of my body.

At first, I welcomed the numbness to my brain, nausea, vomiting, bone pain, and restlessness. It was my punishment for what I had done. The way I went about deceiving the man I love.

Unlike today, everything hurt. It was the one constant in my life that allowed my troubled mind to eventually open up to the new possibilities budding beautifully around me. My therapist taught me that. She made me see the blinding light shining directly in my face. *It is not the end of your world, Lynne. Get up and fight.* Only I was too scared to open my eyes. To see the truth and form a new description of my life.

I chuckle on the inside when my thoughts drift briefly to the first night he slept over.

"Did you still want to go shopping, tomorrow?" I asked.

"Not if I plan on staying here."

I smiled. Jumped up and down on the inside and fell asleep in his arms. Sated. Loved. Not alone.

And now, after spending an entire weekend being worshiped in bed, where I learned my body is extremely pliable when it comes to sex, I hurt in an entirely different way. Between my legs, my inner thighs, and even down to the follicles in my head from being fucked senseless. My hair wrapped around his hand as he pulled and arched my back until he slid slowly inside of me. I will never get enough of him, nor him enough of me.

He's changed. Much more than his controlling ways in bed. Tyson has mellowed out. He talks more. Doesn't hide behind his pain. And some of the things he says will be forever engraved on my soul.

Tyson had every right to drop my father to his knees the other night. He didn't. He backed down. Took a scene that could have gone terribly wrong and walked away. For me.

He's fighting a big change right now. He wants badly to be a part of this. I want that, too. The truth is, Tyson and I are adults. How we handle one another is our business. But these boys, they need to be guided in slowly, gracefully, and with care.

I've become a woman on a mission to beat a man at his own game. Mix my determination with all the talking, sharing, and rediscovering of one another, I found I did not want to climb out of bed this morning no matter how eager I am to move this forward. I wanted to stay there forever. To scatter back to my dreams and not have to do what I'm sitting here doing.

Our weekend has come to an end. It was time to face the world, to get up and go to work. To thank Maggie for what she did for me. To reassure her I honestly was okay. Not to mention, she tried to live vicariously through me by popping into my office every ten minutes trying to pry me into telling her how big Tyson's dick is. I have never laughed so hard in my life, and I owe her so much that my heart swells with more love and thankfulness for her each passing day.

I've done all those things this morning. Now, after sitting here spilling my heart all over the floor, telling Thomas Holder, the attorney Tyson called for me, everything as I sit across from him, I'm frightened he's going to float my happy cloud away. Replace it with a dark gray one that snuck itself in to create a damaging storm and tell me I cannot try and adopt those boys.

"Tyson dropped off this file to me this morning, and I must say I've seen Richard in action in the courtroom, and if your father is that type of man out of the courts as you both claim, he's going to be a tough man to fight here, Lynne." He closes the file, his face holding the same kind of disgust for my father I've held in my heart for years. *Go ahead and speak your mind, Thomas. My father is a disgusting pig.*

"I'm prepared to fight him. Dirty if we have to." My voice is shaky, my insides quake. I relax immediately when Tyson places his hand gently on my thigh and squeezes. He's reminding me I'm not alone anymore. Even though he's here, his constant reassuring words from the weekend where he told me he would be by my side no matter the outcome ringing in my ear, it doesn't stop the fear rolling through me. Nothing will. Not until they are safe in my arms and free from the evil clutches of a man who could destroy them.

"I'd like to propose something first." My pulse skyrockets while I wait for Thomas to tell me his proposal. I'll do anything to keep these children out of this for as long as I can.

"I need you to keep an open mind. To listen to me carefully." He leans forward on his desk, folds his hands in front of him, and slyly smiles when I nod in agreement.

"I suggest we talk to Theo Westbrooke about this. He knows the Hills. He lived there for years. Based on my conversation with Jude this morning, Theo knows your brothers, Lynne. They lived together a few months before Theo moved out."

"What?" I belt out, my hand pressing against my chest. "Theo is a teenager. If my father finds out, he'll just become another target to him. Why didn't you tell me The Hills fostered Theo?" I'm coming off a little harsher than I should, but wow. Talk about a shocking discovery.

"I planned on it. We've been a little preoccupied the past few days. Not going to apologize for something that slipped my mind." He inches his hand all the way up and cups me through my pants. My face heats up. I have no doubt it's turning a bright shade of red right now.

"Right," I squeak, evil-eyeing him with a sideways glance. I'm going to hurt him. Not really. His hand does feel amazing there.

Thomas clears his throat. "Precisely my point. Listen, I've never had the privilege of being the opposition to your father in court. To be able to wipe his arrogance with his own ass. He's conniving, Lynne. You told me this yourself. I've known Jude, Tyson, and Riddick for a long time. They would die before allowing him anywhere near Theo. But those kids, they are unprotected right now, and if your father is a smart man, then he has watchdogs on them. On you. On their house, school. And if he sees you near them, he's going to know." My stomach plummets as I listen to what he's trying not to tell me. He's beating delicately around the bush. It kills me to admit he's right. This could save me from having to expose my family. It would save Jacob and Joshua the humiliation they do not deserve. The hurt they would endure from being rejected.

"Basically, what you're trying to say is, you don't think it's wise for me to be in contact with them?"

"In person, yes. At least until I set up a meeting with the state. Adopting children that have a parent out there who might willingly claim them isn't an easy thing to do, Lynne. It's obvious your father doesn't, but they won't cut corners, not when it comes to the welfare and stability of a child. We have to go about this the right way. I won't deceive the law. I don't think you want to, either." I fall silent. Tyson's hand slips away. So much chaos is circling around in my head. I thought I had done my homework on this. Surely, the state will side with me when they see my father hasn't seen them a day in their lives. Thomas' unspoken words are a sledgehammer to my head. A dissecting breakdown of legalities I didn't put together.

"I don't understand. He's never spoken to them, and he definitely doesn't way them. Surely, the state will side with us on this."

"You would think so. I'm here to work for you. For those kids. I'm not a bullshitter when it comes to being honest with my clients. I want you prepared, not shocked."

"I see. I appreciate that. So, we have to tell them I'm their sister, which means the state will find out who their father is. Did I hear that mixed in there somewhere?"

"No. They will not tell them you're their sister. They will tell them you want to adopt them. Explain to them what it is, how it works. You also know your father. If he doesn't cooperate, then I need more on him than this."

"We're working on that. I have someone watching him. If he's hiding something, we will find it," Tyson adds.

"Good. Keep me posted on what you find out."

I collapse back in my chair; shocked doesn't begin to cover the way I feel by the sudden change of events hitting me out of left field. Tyson told me he has someone watching my father. He's a crooked man. So, hearing him tell Thomas this is no surprise. It's Theo who concerns me right now.

"Did you know about any of this?" I swing my tear-pooled depths toward Tyson. My hands begin to wring in my lap.

"I knew Thomas called Jude about Theo. The rest I put together. I didn't tell you, because you would have worried more than you already did." God, his sentimental eyes sear through me. I'm not angry with him or with Thomas. It's the situation I'm mad at. The protection I've tried hard to provide is going to set back everything I've worked hard to do.

I lean over and place my hand over Tyson's. A reassuring gesture. My heart is embracing itself in a tight grip when he links our hands. His thumb starts caressing my burning skin. I'm so angry with life right now. My father is going to know. He's going to fight me until he thinks he's drained me dry. He will never love those children. He'll do it all out of spite. To me. To Tyson.

"You have yourself a client, Thomas."

***

The weight of the world rests heavily on my shoulders. I'm spending the rest of the day sitting quietly on my deck while watching Cora and Vivian sit merely a football field away as they laugh and encourage Ethan and Riddick to perform tricks on their surfboards. I told myself a hundred times I should walk onto the beach and acknowledge them. I simply don't have it in me to move. My heart is pounding hard, and all I can do is sit as the tears I need to shed fall down my face.

Jude and Theo are gone. They went to see the boys, and I'm frightened that they won't understand why I'm not there telling them myself. Even though Tyson explained to me that my worry was one of the reasons why he didn't tell me right away that Theo lived there, it still doesn't make me feel any better.

I'm worried sick. I want to vomit one minute, and the next say the hell with it and climb in my car and go to them. Explain it all. Tell them I love them and to make sure with my own ears and eyes that they understand.

"Let's go." Tyson's expression is fierce. His words are angered. The anger disappears when he steps out of the house, removes my sunglasses from my face, twirls a strand of my hair, and stares deep into my eyes.

"Go where?" I start to stand only to be held in place with his hand that shifts down to wrap lightly around my neck.

"In the water. Out on the beach with them. Doesn't really matter to me. I'm done watching you sit out here and worry. Everything is going to be fine. I know Jude and Theo. Christ, that boy has been through hell, and look at him, Lynne. He's a good kid with a sensible head on his shoulders. They will tell those boys in a way to make them understand. You sitting out here beating yourself up isn't going to help. Now get up, take that dress off, and get out on the beach." He's right. I know he is. Still, I have my own rights, and right now it's to worry.

"Wow. You are bossy. Did you learn that in the Army?" He directs me a wry smile. Lifts his brows in a way to tell me I haven't seen anything yet. My legs shake, and the aching desire to tumble into the house, straddle him on the floor, and take him inside of me makes me want to dip my fingers in the bottoms of my bikini to see how wet I am.

"Most of it. The rest came from the walls I built up around me. Those walls are a pile of dusty ash now, thanks to you. I may still be bossy. However, when it comes to you, I'll build them back up, only if you agree to be the foundation." Oh, boy. I love it when he can talk the pants right off me without even realizing he does. I choke back a sob. Fill my eyes entirely with all the glory that is Tyson, and lean into his arm. His piercing eyes are glued to his fingers pressing on the pulse at the base of my throat. It consents to his touch, flutters fiercely, and multiplies with a hard, steady beat.

"Tyson. I told the truth the other night when I called you a saint. You are everything to me." His hand grips a tad bit tighter.

"This saint is going to turn into a sinner real fucking quick if you don't move your sexy ass." He drops his hand; I stand and quickly remove my cover-up. Knowing full well that what I have on underneath will turn him into a sinner quicker than me not moving my ass. It's the skimpiest suit I own. Yellow scanty bottoms with a small black lining, a black bandeau top. My breasts practically spill out of it, and the cheeks of my ass hang out of the sides.

"You coming?" I position my hands on my hips, trail my eyes down his bare chest, keeping them steady on the bulge growing inside his swim shorts.

"Not at the moment. I will be soon, though. When I do"—he leans forward and lightly brushes his hand across my breast—"it's going to be all over these."

"Oh." For the moment, I'm all done crying.

***

"He is good. Really good." I haven't a clue what it is I'm watching Riddick and Tyson do out of the corner of my eye as they shove one another like teenage boys under the water. My radar is solely focused on Ethan.

"He is. He knows it, too," Cora agrees. I lean back onto the blanket, dig my elbows in for leverage, and watch Cora and Vivian take the young man in. It's clear to see how much that boy is adored and loved. It pains me all over again not to know what it will feel like to have a child grow inside of me. To feel him or her move, to hear the steady rhythm of a heartbeat. All of it vanishes with the wind when Cora quietly speaks her mind. Her opinion striking closer to home than she realizes.

"What you are doing for those boys is one of the most self-sacrificing things I've heard of, Lynne. It proves to us all that you will be a wonderful mother." Happiness crawls through my veins. A smile creeps across my face. It's true. I'm going to be a wonderful mother once I have them.

"I agree. We all do. Jude and Theo especially. We want to help you, Lynne. Anything you need from us we will give."

"You two are the best," I mutter. "Hearing you say these things to me means so much. I'm not sure what any of us can do at this point. It's out of my hands until I hear back from the state or my delightful father decides to show up again and ruin everyone's night. The thought of you wanting to help is enough for me. And for you accepting me into your lives, showing me what friends and family are all about. I don't think anyone will truly understand what that alone means to me."

"If he knows what's good for him, he won't show his face around here again. And we do understand. Don't we, girls?" A voice speaks from behind me. One I recognize from the hallways of the hospital to the short time I talked to her the other night. Sylvia Shepard.

A string of emotions rises fast like the swells in the sea inside of me when Cora's parents open up chairs and plop right down beside me. Maggie and her grandsons are on the other side. It's such a beautiful sight. A stage set for a photograph from behind. A family all in a row with me right in the middle.

"Yes, we do," they both answer in unison.

Tyson told me all about Cora, Riddick, and Ethan over the weekend. My heart crashed hard into my ribs for all of them. What a horrible nightmare to have to live through.

Let's hope we can finally escape all our nightmares.

CHAPTER FIFTEEN

TYSON

"Where is she?" I keep my head down, tighten the last bolt on the wooden beach swing us guys built for the women, and cringe from the screeching, high-pitched voice hollering at me. My hands clench at my sides. I recognize that tone. It sounds just like her sister. The sarcastic thing is, Lynne's voice is full of kindness, whereas this voice has malicious animosity dripping from the fangs ready to suck the blood out of you. It shrieks spoiled brat. Goddamn. I hate these fucking people.

Lynne has blocked them all from her phone. Tossed every photograph in a box and swears she feels less emotional stress, and here comes the killer princess to try and cause her havoc. I know damn well Richard passed on the message that she is done with all of them. My guess is, she's here for her own selfish reasons. Her mother sent her to do her dirty work. I'll bet my ass on it. Hell, I'd bet my life. She probably doesn't have a clue what the fuck it is he's done. Wouldn't matter to Laney anyway when all she cares about is what it's going to look like. Dumb-ass bitter bitch.

It's been a little over a week since we went to see Thomas. Every time we call, he tells us the same damn thing. "It's the state. They move on their time." I don't think they realize that we don't have time. This isn't a normal adoption. Lynne should be able to jump right through the hoops of every law invented to adopt a foster child. They are her brothers, for fuck's sake.

The problem with all of that is, her father could be ten steps ahead of us before the state even lets us know.

She's been going out of her mind with worry. Even though Jude and Theo came back with the best news for her, she still is. Those kids want to be with her so bad that they begged the Hills to talk to Lynne.

The genius that Jude is made it happen. They've been video chatting nonstop. Even I've met them on screen and Christ, they are wonderful.

They look so much alike it's crazy, and yet every time I see them, I know which one is which.

Their personalities are different. They both love to talk, except I noticed Jacob uses his hands when he does, whereas Joshua tends to be so loud Lynne is constantly telling him to lower his voice. That's one of the reasons for this swing. He can be as loud as he wants to be out here playing while she watches them. There's another thing I noticed about them right away, too. Jacob's eyes are a darker shade of green than his brother's, and thank fuck they resemble their biological mother more than they do Richard. I mean, you can see him in them, but Lynne was right when she said they are nothing like that bastard at all.

On top of all of that, she's been working her ass off at her office. Patients are booking, and she's even negotiating a contract with the hospital to be on call one night a week for emergency situations.

I sigh, glance up to Jude and Tyson, who are now walking toward me with beers in their hands and deep frowns on their faces. It's obvious they don't like our visitor, either.

"Tyson, please tell us where she is. She's our sister. We're worried about her." Ah, so both of her bitchy-ass sisters decided to show up. This voice sounds more like their mother. Straight up bitch. Thank God, all the women are off doing whatever the hell women do. Shopping and nails. Hell, I have no clue. As long as Lynne continues to smile every day, she can go off and do whatever the hell she wants. But these soul suckers here, they will never speak to her again if I have my way about it.

"Her sisters?" Jude queries, bends his head to stare them down over his glasses, and passes me a beer. I nod.

Taking a long swig, I finally turn toward them, lift my shirt, and wipe the sweat off my face. I'm dirty as fuck, smell just as bad, and they couldn't have picked a better time to show up here. They think I'm the thin layer of scum floating around on top of the water. Well, I'm about to show them that I own the whole dirty-ass pond.

"It's obvious she isn't here. If she were, you'd be gone already." I can see them both rolling their eyes from where I stand. Bitches. The fucker inside of me wants to verbally call them that and so much more. But the man in me taps it down. Now, if her mother were with them, I'd call her and these little minions a hell of a lot worse than bitches.

"They afraid to get their shoes dirty or what?" I bust out laughing at Jude's comment. One look at them and he has them pegged.

"It appears so. I bet those thousand-dollar shoes are perfectly lined up on the edge of the grass. God forbid the witches get sand in their shoes," I sputter. These women have always brought out the worst in me. Never could stand either one of them.

"Well, can you at least tell us if she's…"

"If she's what? Alright? Depressed? Climbed back in her hole? I'm not telling you shit, except to get the hell out of here. She doesn't want anything to do with you. What part of that don't you understand? For fuck's sake, leave her alone. She's finally living. I'm so sick of this shit coming from you people that I'm about ready to start slapping people upside the heads."

And she is living. In spite of her being worried, Lynne is blossoming in every direction. Especially with Cora and Vivian. I've never seen her this happy, and I'll continue to be the son of a bitch I am to make sure she stays that way. I'm tired of this shit. It's messing with my head. Women or not, if they have the guts to show up here, then they better accept what's going down. They aren't getting anywhere near her. Not one of them.

"We're her sisters. We love her. We've done nothing for her to cut us out of her life." Hearing Larissa say that causes me to snap. I'm going to rain the wrath of hell on them. They can take it right back to their parents for all I care.

"I'm going to say this one time. I suggest you listen." I stalk their way. My eyes feral. My body is all kinds of tensed up. "You have no control here. In fact, you do not exist after today. Love isn't a convenience. It doesn't come with a price tag that deflates your wallet or your time. It doesn't come with one at all. It's freely given. And neither one of you have given it to her. If you loved her, you would have known the hell she went through. You would have put a stop to what your parents did to her, and she would be my wife. Jesus Christ, what the hell is wrong with all of you?" I don't even flinch when tears start streaming down Larissa's face. I know she's been the only one who has tried to make peace within her family. Peace isn't what Lynne needed. She needed them to stand up for her. She needed her fucking sisters.

They both take several steps back as if my words slapped them across their face. I hope they run back home scared. Tell Daddy I attacked them, too.

"Is she happy?" Larissa asks.

"That's none of your business."

"It most certainly is. Our mother won't leave her house. She's worried." This is coming from Laney. She's so much like her mother it literally makes me sick.

"Do you really think I don't have anything up here to know what the fuck you all are trying to do?" I point to my head. "It was my business years ago when she had cancer. You sure the fuck weren't worried about her then. Did you make it my business? Did you come and find me so I could help her? Fuck, no, you didn't. I'm going to tell you the same thing I told your father when he stepped onto this property. If you ever come back here again, I'll toss your asses in jail. Leave her alone. We do not want you here. She's tired of you interfering, and this time there isn't a thing any of you can do to rip us apart. For God's sake. Get a clue. You can leave now. I'm done wasting my time on you. And ask your mother to tell you the truth about why she isn't leaving her house." I turn my back on them the same way they did her. I head straight to the ocean, where Jude and Riddick are, knowing full well they'll be gone when I turn around. The part of me that loves Lynne wishes they would stick around and show Lynne they truly do love her. They won't. *Our mother is worried about her.* Who the hell do they think they're talking to? Ellen won't leave because she scared Lynne will run to the press if all hell breaks loose. Dumb as a fucking rock. Every last one of them.

"Damn. This situation is similar to Cora's in certain ways yet different. How can people come from the same set of parents and one be loving and caring, while the rest are made up of evil?"

"I wish I knew, Riddick. If I did, our women wouldn't have gone through hell," I respond.

"I don't get why everyone is so hell-bent on talking to her. It's driving me fucking crazy trying to figure this family out. I can't find a damn thing on any of them. Other than Richard's infidelity."

Something about that word 'infidelity' doesn't sit well with me. It's a nagging intuition that drives me to ask Jude to step up his game one more time.

"Jude, brother. I need you to do something for me, and I need it quick."

***

"Thank you for sticking up for me today." I shoot Lynne an arrogant grin, then grab her by her ass and tug her down to me. Her long legs straddle my hips. Her hair in those two short, messy braids is making my brain go straight to the gutter.

I wanted to wait until after dinner after we had our nightly chat with the boys to drop this shit on her. She knew something was wrong the minute she walked through the door with several bags of items she bought at some second-hand store she loves. Entirely different than the women who stepped out of their fancy-ass car today.

That's the thing about her and me. One of the many things time can't erase. Simply put, we know each other, and when something is weighing heavily on the other person's mind, everything else waits. Whatever is bothering us, we were always putting that first. That will never change.

I asked Jude to check into something for me. This something could lift the last nail in Lynne's coffin if my notion is spot-on. She could finally be free of every last one of them. Move the fuck on and we can start our lives together. Me, her, and the kids. My gut is telling me I have this all figured out. The guys, too, after I told them what was rumbling inside of my head. Now I feel guilty as fuck for not sharing this with her. I can't do it. Not until I know for sure. So, right now, I'm thankful her sisters showed up. Keeps us both distracted from what's really pondering away on my mind.

I meant it when I said she's unbreakable. She is. But this will prove it more than anything. It will show her that she has the upper hand. That she can call their bluff and beat them at a game she's been trailing behind in for years. It will shut them all up. For good.

"They'll be back. I'm sure of it." I grab her ass and grind my cock into her pussy. My attention going back to her.

She lets out a deep sigh. Frowns for a split second and presses her body into me. God, she feels so good. Here in my arms. Our devotion to see our lives become one hanging in the thick pull of the air. No matter what happens, I got her.

"I'm sure they will. Either that or I'll see them in court. I don't want to talk about them anymore. They don't exist, remember?" I remember, alright. It's her I'm worried about. She claims it doesn't bother her when I know it does. Lynne may have it in her to despise her parents, but her sisters? Not so much.

"I don't have an issue with you having a relationship with them." Biggest lie I've ever told.

"Tyson. I will always care about them, but no. When this all comes out, they will be on his side. They haven't changed one bit. They didn't come here because they care about me. They came here to upset me. I mean it. I'm better off without them all. In the little time I've had to get to know Cora and Vivian, they've made up for all I've lost with Larissa and Laney. I don't need them. I need you. The boys. Our family. Trust me." Right there I remind myself why I fell in love with her in the first place. She has a heart so full of love to give you can't help but gravitate toward her. The same goes for all the women in our lives. It sucks her family can't see that. Sucks for them, because they honestly have no clue what they are missing.

"I love you." Those three words easily come out of nowhere. I've been dying to tell her. To hear her say it back to my face. Now seems like the best time to tell her. It has nothing to do with her family. Nothing to do with anyone except her and me.

Love doesn't even come close to what I feel for her. There isn't a word to describe it. There's nothing stronger, purer than falling so deep that it's the only thing in your life that you are sure of.

A smile as bright as the sun soars across her beautiful face. Every one of her smiles seems to be better than the last. She unmans me with them. Leaves marks all over me when I see happiness settling deep in her bones.

Dark green eyes glisten back at me. I wait. My breath is floating between the thin space separating my mouth from hers.

"I've waited and dreamed for so long to hear you say that. I love you more than anything, Tyson Corelli." Christ. My dick. Hanging by a string. Pulled. Toward her.

"I know, baby." In time, I hope I can call her a Corelli. Maybe have a couple twins running around this house with the same last name. Time will tell. We have so much of it now.

"This isn't moving too fast for us, is it?" She sighs, eyes open big and wide.

"Fuck, no. It's been moving around the orbit for long enough. Besides, I could give a shit what others think. This is our story. Everyone else can go fuck themselves."

"I think I heard something similar to that not long ago." She giggles. Grinds down on me and slides her hands up my arms. Wrapping them around my neck.

I'm content. At ease. And then she ups the ante when her fingers skim down my chest, twine around my back and straight into the band of my shorts.

"These need to come off." They sure the hell do.

She scoots back a hair, slips her hands to cup my ass, and I lift enough to help her guide them down. Her eyes are erotically wild. When she licks her lips, my cock can't help but leap into a straight-up standing position. He's more than ready for her attention. Eager as fuck to have her wrap those lips around him and suck.

"Jesus. Fuck," I roar. My head is instantly slamming back against the couch when she cups my balls and rolls them. She slides the rest of the way off me. My fucking head lolls to the side when I see her head dive down, her mouth open up, and her tongue start sliding up my length.

Tranced. Every damn time.

"Lynne." She ignores me. Her fingers are wrapping around my base. He mouth is in tune with her hand as she starts a wicked little game of hand-mouth combo on my dick. Up then down in synced momentum.

I don't think she realizes what she does to me. The power she has and holds. Christ Almighty. If she stops right now, I'm going to lose one hell of an orgasm.

"Not going to bullshit, Lynne. Your mouth is driving me insane. Won't take but a few more minutes and I'm going off down your throat. Don't think for a damn minute we're stopping there, either." She glances up at me with eyes as bright as a stick of dynamite about to go off. They are on fucking fire.

"Shit," I groan. My balls are squeezing tight in the palm of her hand. She knows how to play, to win, and I'm fighting like a bull not to grab her braids, yank her head back, and come all over her tits.

I roar out her name when the urge to release hits me hard. My body goes still. Everything around me fades away. Except her. The woman on her knees in front of me.

"Get up here, dirty girl."

CHAPTER SIXTEEN

LYNNE

"Joshua, buddy, slow down. I can't understand what you're trying to say," I encourage around a subdued laugh. Burrowing further into Tyson's side, I rest my head on his shoulder to hide the big smile etching its way across my face. Joshua is trying so hard to tell me something, but the excitement inside of him is causing his words to jumble altogether. It's the most adorable thing I've seen.

Another two days have gone by with no word from the state, no unwanted visitors. I'm losing my mind over this.

"We're listening, buddy," Tyson tosses in. I peer up at him. He's so content, laid-back when it comes to these boys that it irritates the heck out of me. How the heck he can keep a straight face right now is beyond me. So annoying.

He's completely infatuated with these kids. I knew he would be. You can't help but fall for them. They are everything. A bright light, an answer to prayers. Lately, though, I've been keeping my guard up. Doing all I can to safeguard my heart, just in case Jacob and Joshua are pulled away from me without a choice from any of us. I'm way over my head, my heart is committed to this, and my gut is telling me something terribly unexpected is about to happen.

I sit up, lay my hand across Tyson's knee, and give Joshua my undivided attention.

Joshua huffs out a breath, rolls his eyes, and places his cute little face right up to the screen. Gosh, I want to lean in like a blubbering fool and pull him into my arms. Jacob too. If only I could. I miss seeing them in person so much.

"You need to listen to me, Lynne," he speaks in a growly little voice. "It's called 'Milk for Moms.' Will you come with us?" Oh, my freaking God.

"Really? When is it?" I may have stuttered those words out from the wish galloping through me right now. I want to tell him yes right away. The world suddenly skids to a halt, allowing the word 'mom' to catch up. The emotions inside of me are running wild and crazy. I would love nothing more than to do this with them.

The laughter fades away, the tears of joy want to express themselves, and I find myself sinking back into my couch, leaving a little boy waiting for his answer.

"Mrs. Stedman gave us the papers in school. She said it was next month." Jacob appears on the screen holding two pieces of paper in his hand. He places them up for me to see, and my world fades away. It scrambles around, balancing itself in order for me to think like a normal human instead of someone who has been given a shock to her system.

"She would love to go, guys, what's the other paper for?" Tyson lifts the laptop off the table and places it on his lap.

I'm flabbergasted. Partially numb and angry. They want me to go with them to this event at their school? *Mom.* That word is doing somersaults inside of my heart. It's singing for joy and fist-pumping in the air. The thing is, and there always seems to be a thing, a factor, or a big problem of a certain someone in my way of making this an actuality for me. Right now, that damn factor is the state. There has to be a way to bend the law without necessarily breaking it. *When will this end?*

"Heck, yeah, I'll go. We'll work it all out with Mrs. Hill. Talk to you guys tomorrow."

He'll what? My anger erupts. "You'll go where?" I probe. My own frustration is punching me in the gut.

"Dairy with Dads" He closes the laptop, tosses it on the other side of the couch, and reaches for me.

"No." I jerk out of his grasp. Push off of the couch and glare at him.

"You shouldn't have told them you would go. We can't promise them that. They might not even be here in a month. We don't know what's going to happen and you can't go around promising them things that may not come true."

"I can do whatever the hell I want. There isn't anyone going to tell me I can't go with them. No one, Lynne." Oh, God. Now he's angry, too. Good. I'm not ignoring how much hearing him say that means to me. My heart is swimming in a pool full of bliss over it. It's just…we have to be careful, and he knows this.

"Tyson, what is wrong with you?" I snap. The second those words are out of my mouth, I wish I could shove them back and choke on them. Except I can't. The more I think about it, I shouldn't have to, and I'm not apologizing for them, either. "You've been distant all day. There's something bothering you other than this, and I want to know what it is."

He has been. I know him too well. Tyson and I have spent every free moment together these past few weeks. We've talked for hours. We've made love daily, nightly. Sometimes several times a day. We cannot get enough of each other.

At first, I thought it might have something to do with his job. He doesn't tell me much about it because he can't. I understand all too well the confidentiality he has to keep. I'm not allowed to tell him certain things, either. But this, whatever it is that's bothering him, has nothing to do with his job. It has to do with me. With this case. And I'm going out of my mind trying to figure it out.

"Lynne, come here."

"No. I'm not giving in to your bossiness this time, Tyson. It's been two weeks and not a word from the state. My family has quit calling the office. They haven't unexpectedly stopped by, and I know my father better than anyone. They've contacted him by now; I know they have." *Oh, God.* I have too much going on in my head again. I'm drowning in it, and I can't take it anymore.

Since we started this process, I've been waiting for the shoe not only to drop; I've been waiting for the damn thing to start beating me in the head. I'm worried, frustrated, and angry, eager. Most of all, I'm afraid my father really hates me that much that he'll do whatever it takes to knock me down until I can't get up.

Silence from a man like my father is more harming to me that his constant meddling in my life. It's scaring the shit out of me.

"You need to calm the hell down. I'm on your side, baby. Not his. Yours, the boys'. Taking your aggravation out on me is only going to lead to us fighting, and I refuse to let that happen. Is that what you want? To argue, lash out at me? If it is, then you can have at it with the four walls in this house, because I'm not going to be a part of it." He shoves off the couch, grabs his bottle of water, and storms out the door. I stand there with my mouth hanging open, wondering what in the hell just happened. How did we go from our usual conversation with the kids to engaging in a battle on opposite sides?

"Hello." I close my mouth up and turn my head to see Maggie, Vivian, and Cora at my door. Even though I love them all dearly, the idea of having company right now is low on my feel-sorry-for-myself scale.

"What are you three up to?" I ask, putting on my usual mask of normalcy. These no-bullshit ladies see through it every damn time, though. Each one of them calls me out when I sink back into myself. I love them. My sisters. My family.

I push the screen door open for them to enter and stand there staring blankly at the screen when it closes behind them. Wishing Tyson would come back. And then it all hits me at once. The gloominess is gone. The sky a bright blue. Tyson put this screen door on; he put one on each of the French doors, so the breeze would flow through the house. He's done so much in such a short period of time. Not only to this house but for me. He's been by my side; he's called the state. Went above and beyond to try and push things ahead for me, and I just dumped it all over his head as if none of it mattered.

"Hey, what's going on, honey?" Maggie asks, amusement dancing in her eyes. It's not funny. If I hadn't somehow found my strength through all of this, I would break down and cry right now. I have found it. It's such a fulfillment. I've learned to love myself, forgive and shove it all behind me. Just like Tyson suggested I do. And even though it was me making up my own mind to do it, he gave me that push I needed to shove me in the direction I desperately needed to go.

"I think we had our first fight," I mutter.

"I see. And what? You're standing here blaming yourself?" I circle around to face them all. Of course, Vivian would be the one with her hip jutted out, her eyes rolling after her little ball of information. Cora looks a tad bit sympathetic, and Maggie is now smirking.

"Well, yeah. It was me who started it." I shrug, narrow my eyes at Vivian. She's far from done with expressing herself. This woman is a handful for me to keep up with. Even though she's partially right. I shouldn't blame myself. It takes two to argue. It only takes one to admit they were wrong. To end it and move on. Not sure if that makes sense, but I'm going with it.

"So what? Make it you who finishes it. Give him time to cool off and then apologize. Tell him you love him and then fuck his brains out. Works for me every time." *My thoughts exactly, Vivian, as soon as I figure out a way to apologize.*

"Vivian. Not everyone is like you. We don't know what they argued about." Cora understands my past more than anyone. We have talked, and as a result of our many talks, she has become extremely dear to me. I fit in with all of them, really. We shop, we get pedicures, and we laugh, drink, and enjoy each other's company so much that my family really ceases to exist. Except they don't. They are all waiting with pitchforks and shovels in their bloody little hands, just holding up on the edge of the hole to bury me. I know they are.

"Whatever, Cora. Look, Lynne. It is none of our business what you argued about. I'm not suggesting you tell us. What I should have said is, everyone argues. It's healthy. At least I think it is. Arguing means there is communication. It shows you both have your opinions. Don't fault yourself for that. If you feel it was your fault, then tell him that. Ask him to forgive you and move on."

"Wow. If you ever lose your job at the hospital, you can come work for me." I smile jokingly.

"Maybe I will. Seriously, though. You'll find it makes the bond the two of you have stronger."

"Things will work out, Lynne. You two have come back to one

another. Fights are going to happen. Here, this should make you happy."
Maggie pulls a small little box out of her beach bag. It's wrapped in
the prettiest shade of pink paper with a tiny little white bow on top.
It reminds me of the pink box that I stored my engagement ring from
Tyson in. I have it in a box under my bed. The blanket, my ring, and
pictures of the two of us were the only things I took with me when I left
for my surgery and chemotherapy. Tyson didn't have much money to
buy me things. Not that I complained. Our love is true, and to me, that
means more than anything money can buy.

"You didn't have to buy me anything. Your friendship is all I need,"
I say excitedly.

"We didn't buy it. Well, that's partially true. Maggie made it. Vivian,
our mom, and I added to it. Open it. I think it will make you feel better.
Give you the courage to go make up with your man." Cora lifts her
brows. I smile, tentative at first. My head is reeling with the possibilities
of what could possibly be inside. I slide the bow off, lift up the lid, and
gasp.

"This is… it's perfect." I hold up the silver bracelet similar to another
one Maggie gave me for my birthday shortly after we met. She makes
them. How she does it I will never know. It's her special design, she calls
it. A hidden talent. The one she gave me has a little seashell dangling
where this one has two hearts soldered together.

"Read them," Cora pushes, the three of them circling around me.
I squint my eyes, let out a noise somewhere between a cry and an all-
out sob when I read the word 'family' on both sides. I flip them over,
revealing 'sister' on one and 'daughter' on the other. I don't know what
to say. All my words are lost to me now. The last time I received a gift
that meant so much to me was the engagement ring from Tyson. Blood
doesn't mean family. And it sure as hell might be thicker than water but
it thins out the minute it leaves our veins.

"No tears, damn it. You've cried enough. Here." Maggie takes the
bracelet, outstretches my hand, and guides it up to settle comfortably
right next to the other.

"Thank you," I acknowledge, finally finding my voice.

These women get me. They find me at my weakest and literally smack me over the head with kindness. I felt so alone before they all came into my life and now I feel stronger. Like I could do anything I set my heart on. I've always considered myself to be a weak woman when the truth is, I've never been. I'm strong. Worth so much more than I've believed I deserved.

"You're welcome. We mean this. You are part of the family. No matter what, Lynne. Always remember that."

***

"I'm sorry, Tyson. It wasn't fair of me to take my emotions out on you." I sit down next to him on the beach. The water is lapping inches away from our toes.

"We're going to argue, Lynne. Hell, you'll probably want to punch me most of the time. This is us getting to know each other again. It's me and you figuring out how to make a life for ourselves. It's us finally being happy. To wash away a tainted past that we both thought would eventually be the death of us. This is all getting to me, too. I'm not mad at you. It's this whole fucked-up situation that has me pissed off. We all handle our shit differently. You've been through so much of it. It's my right to protect you from not dealing with any more. I do have something to share with you. It's been eating away at me for two days."

My heart is not a fan of the torment behind his eyes. I gulp, fear rioting with pain over which one is going to win out when he reveals what's obvious to see is killing him.

I link out hands together. Prepared to protect him in the same way he does me. Love brings that out in a person. It shields, it defends. Even though my insides are quivering and the notion I had earlier of something brewing on the horizon is hanging on the words he has yet to speak, I can handle it. For there is nothing in this world I won't do to save our souls from drifting apart again.

CHAPTER SEVENTEEN

TYSON

"Tell me, Tyson. You're scaring me. I'm tired of being scared, so just say it," she urges.

Lynne stares back at me intensely. She knows that whatever is eating away at me is ripping my gut out. It's killing me in ways I can't come up with the right way to deliver this news. I wait, my pulse tapping away at my brain, every bang slamming down harder until it's rapping so hard I do everything in my power to block up, to smash it away with a hard blast of my own.

To hell with it. I need to let it rip. Spill it and take care of her if she needs me to.

"After your sisters left here last week, I asked Jude to look into something for me. Don't ask me why the thought ran through my mind; it just did. Lynne, Richard isn't your biological father. Your mother had an affair. In fact, I found out who your real father is."

Fifteen minutes ago, I was sitting here talking to Jude. My anger at Lynne lashing out at me gone. Honestly, I was never mad at her. How the hell could I be when both of us are standing in the same anger-filled shoes?

And now, as I stare into eyes turning a steely green, the heated anger is begging Lynne to let go. I'm not afraid that what we found out wasn't the right thing to do. It was, and God help her. Once this news settles in, she needs to plow right through the hurt wanting to consume her and let anger manage this. See it for what it is. It's a miracle.

Everything she wondered about her being so different from him is right. She is not Richard's child.

"It's about damn time she blew up. She needs to do it more often. I'd rather she took her anger out on someone other than me. Preferably, her fucked-up, dysfunctional family. The problem is, I get why she did. Unlike her, though, I'm not sitting around waiting any longer. If the state doesn't bust their ass to get them into a permanent home, then I'll do it for them. I'll be damned if I'll allow anyone to make decisions for her or for me again. Jacob and Joshua want us there, Jude." I glance up at Jude facing me. His back is blocking the sun from hitting my eyes.

I had to walk out before I told her what's been eating me alive out of my own frustration. Ran down the beach a ways and caught Jude on a run with his dogs. Now, here I sit envisioning Lynne pounding the hell out of her mother, while I do the same with her father. Childish, but I'd be lying to myself if the idea hasn't crossed my mind. A lot.

"I know, brother. I swear I'm putting as much pressure on the caseworker who helped me with Theo as I can. It has to be her father stalling. She sure has had her string of bad luck, though. This information is going to bring it all to an end. What we did is not only the best for her; it's the right thing for those kids, too. It gives her another wage to stake. A bigger one."

"I know you are. Couldn't thank you more for it. That right there, though, is what's pissing me off more than anything. The mere fact that he has a say in this at all is so far out of whack I can see why people bitch about the system. Lynne needs to learn the odds. How to place her bet in her favor. I wish like hell I didn't have to say this, but man, Lynne and I are going to have to go see those dirty, leeching humans. Not sure if I can stomach being that close to either one of them and not want to choke all their lies and deceit out of them. The big problem I'm having here is, there's no guarantee she's going to win, Jude. Richard could laugh in her face. I mean, shit, look at what this means. She has no legal ground to stand on when it comes to them anymore. Her highest card is her mother, and we all know Ellen hasn't used her ace she's been hiding for over thirty years. I don't fucking get these people. Hell, why would

Richard raise another kid that wasn't his? Why would they all want to live in misery? This is fucked up. It makes no sense, and I can't make heads or tails of any of it."

"It's greed for their reputation, Tyson. All of this simmers down to it. Here she comes. You two will figure it out. I'm heading in to take a shower. I'll catch you later, yeah?" He pats my shoulder, gathers up his dogs, and leaves me to my own thoughts.

I'd breezed through the last couple of days with work. Placing what we learned in check. Sorting my shit out and solely focusing on Lynne until I couldn't do it anymore.

The first thing I did once Jude confirmed my suspicions was head right to my captain, filled him in on what was going on and again asked for some time off. He didn't tell me to come back with my head pulled out of my ass the way he did when I told him I needed to get out of town when Lynne walked back into my life. He told me to fix the shit. That my track record spoke volumes at work and my loyalty to her showed him the man inside of me I kept hidden for years. A good man. Made me feel as if I'd been a walking son of a bitch toward everyone. I suppose I was. I sure as fuck didn't truly care about my own damn self, so caring about everyone else around me didn't mean shit to me, either.

But he, like Riddick and Jude, Dane, and Dominic, has proven to me that seeing a person underneath is worth sticking around for. That somewhere behind my dark mask lies a better man. A man who will have a person's back no matter the outcome.

I went back to my apartment. Worked from there and dug up the courage to call a man I never knew existed. I waited for hours for him to call me back, and when he did, I dropped a bomb on him. Not once caring if it exploded. All I cared about was finding a way to move this forward for her. To be able to give her peace.

It seemed insulting as fuck when we learned who he was, what he used to do for a living, and how he never owned up to being her father. I wanted to slice his tongue out of his mouth and shove it up his bullshitting ass, up till he told me his story, flinging my shit right back at me.

He never fucking knew. And I loathed her mother more for not doing right by her daughter. For leaving me to be the one to tell him he had a daughter. Doesn't mean a thing that she has yet to find out I know. But she will. Soon. And I'm going to watch her drown in her scum-filled pond as I brush her and her family out of Lynne's life forever.

At first, I didn't believe him. I figured he would deny it. Hide behind himself the same way her mother has been doing. But nope, not a chance in hell. He's a man who isn't afraid to uncheck his man card. To cry over the phone to a complete stranger and thank him for being man enough to tell him something he had a right to know.

Retired NYPD Police Sergeant Matthew Sauder. College roommate to none other than Richard Chapman. A best friend who slipped one night and slept with Lynne's mother.

He claimed he was in town visiting and back then Ellen was kind, gentle, and a total sweetheart. I'll never be a believer of it; it's irrelevant at this point. They were sitting around drinking while waiting for Richard to come home. Things got heated, she advanced on him, and he fucked her. That one night resulted in Lynne.

And fuck all if I'm not sitting here after dumping a life-changing collision that could change the course of Lynne's dream in any direction.

That bitch is clever. Even more so than her husband. This could fuck shit up, or it could calm it down.

"I'm not sure if I need to sit here and regroup myself, ask you a million questions, or finally turn into a bitch on wheels and kill them for keeping this from me. Honestly, the thought never crossed my mind that she could have done something to taint her reputation this way. It all makes perfect sense. Richard knows I'm not his. This is why he's treated me as if I'm beneath his shoe and when I became sick, he took that as his sign to pay me back for being born. Oh, God, I feel sick. She… my mother went along with it. How could she do such a thing? I thought I hated them before, but that was nothing compared to what I feel for them now. This explains everything, Tyson." I'm doing my best to put up a calm front for her. To let this sink in when all I want to do is start shooting people and relieving her pain from them existing to be able to hurt her anymore. Every last one of them should be swept off this earth. Fall to hell and suffer.

"You have every right to be angry, but don't you dare give them the satisfaction of making yourself ill. They don't deserve anything from you, except to bury them alive with their own deception." The color that started to drain from her face returns; it contorts into a red ball of fury. I'm hoping she becomes so angry at them that she bursts from it. That she pulls their holy rug from under them and when she's ready allows her newfound DNA running through her blood to help.

She closes her eyes, takes several deep breaths, and squeezes my hand tighter. "Who is he?" she asks. The raw hurt in her tone pisses me the fuck off, and yet for the time being it's calming down the maniac in me, too.

I've never met this man, but I'll be damned if he didn't get on the first plane he could to prove to me his loyalty to a child he never knew was his.

"Before I tell you, you need to know he didn't know you were his."

"Well, I would hope not. I really don't think I could handle knowing there was someone out there who knew I was their child and didn't step up. It would make him just like Richard. You talk as if I know him. Do I?" Her brows furrow, forehead wrinkles in that way we all do when we're trying to figure something out.

"Exactly, and he's not. At least I don't believe he is." I need to tell her I know who he is and so does she before she goes completely mad, giving her the chance to freak the hell out about what this could mean for her and Joshua and Jacob. This is the part that angers me the most. I can't protect her from this. It's not my right to do so. Only he can. It's his story. Her story. And fuck, I pray that he stands by her side. Holds her hand and gives her the one thing in life she's always wanted. To be loved by a parent.

"It's me." I take hold of her upper arm when her body locks up, the muscles beneath my grip tense and constrict. I can't help but shift my head, angling it enough to be able to glare at him standing behind us.

"Couldn't wait any longer to take a look at my daughter in a way a father should." He shrugs, gives me a look that tells me he doesn't give a fuck what I told him to do. I asked him to wait for me to tell her. To give Lynne the chance to come to him if she wanted. Guess I pegged this man for the true guy he is. He's not going to deny himself any longer to stand by his daughter's side. To help her fight.

"Holy shit. Matthew? He's my father?" She still hasn't looked at him. Her gaze is trained on me to confirm it.

"Yeah, baby, he is. We can run blood tests to prove it if you want." I release my hold on her arm, slide it up her neck to run my thumb back and forth across her trembling bottom lip. "Don't cry. Take your time. This is a good thing for you. You have someone who loves you unconditionally, Lynne. Breathe, okay?"

I stay rooted to my spot and witness this incredible woman who has been through hell her entire life slowly push herself up. Deep breaths escape her mouth. Her focus trained on the ocean. One would assume at a time such as this that tension would fill the air, that dark clouds would form up above, and a storm would drop pounding rain, pelting hail, and thunder would roll across her tormented features. I see none of that. What I do see is a bright beacon of light, a ghost of a smile as the perceptiveness of what this means to her strikes a shocking surge of lightning.

"Lynne." Matthew slowly moves forward; she closes her eyes as her chest rises and falls.

Slowly. So damn slowly, she braces herself, turns around, and opens them. No tears, no pain. Not more unforgiving conceptions burn in the beauty that has always surrounded her. I'm invading on an intimate moment. I'll be damned if I'll go, or If I'll leave fate to allow me to miss this cherished memory of her life.

"My God, Matthew. I can't believe this. You're here."

"Of course, I am. I came as soon as I could. It's been a long time, sweetheart. You look wonderful. More beautiful than you were the last time I saw you." She studies him, her lips parting as if she wants to say something. Ask him questions. Feel him out. I don't know.

"Do you remember when I would come to visit? How I would always bring you girls a gift?" He reaches into his pocket and pulls something out. No matter how much I want to stay here in case she falls apart, I can't. She's safe. She's loved. And as I stand up to leave, I see his hand open wide. His eyes remain focused on her.

"You always asked me to bring you one of these. A Statue of Liberty eraser. I'm going to help you erase your past with this. And we're going to sketch the life you deserve with this." He opens up his other hand, which holds a pencil.

I hear her gasp as I begin to walk away. I'm unmanned. I'm undone. And I couldn't give a fuck if the wetness forming in my eyes portrays me as weak. Real men cry. They wear just as many emotions on their sleeves as everyone else.

***

"Fucking hell," I roar, peering over the edge of Riddick's roof. A bottle of water in my hand, a cigar in the other.

When my shitty life would sucker-punch me in the gut over and over until I could barely breathe, I always went for the bottle. The hard stuff to disorient my conscious mind. To deliver the evil that enlarged my veins enough to burst into a state of unconsciousness. Not today, though. Not ever again. I won't do a damn thing to jeopardize Lynne getting those kids. I only hope the confidence I have in myself, the faith I have in my brothers, their women, and my extended family that are all watching Lynne and Matthew stroll back into our view from being gone for hours was the right thing to do. I only need her.

Their shadows are encroached by darkness. And yet I know it's them. I feel her presence coming back to me with every step they take.

"Dude, maybe you should stay up here and let me go check on her."

"Shut up, Jude." I chuckle lightly over the nonsense spewing out of his mouth. It's similar to what I told him when Vivian came back. Only I'm not staying up here. I'm going to my girl.

"Yeah, that's what I thought," he says to my retreating back as I throw my empty bottle at him and descend the stairs. All of their laughter trickling away behind me.

"Are you alright?" I place my palms on her cheeks, looking closely into her bright green eyes. It seems like forever ago when the same reflection stared back at me the night I asked her to marry me. Bright as a star. Her eyes, her lips, and her spirit shine the same way. All at once. I tug her into me. Having no idea how I made it through thirteen years without worrying to death over her. She's been in a safety net for two hours, and I've gone out of my mind.

"Tyson. I'd like you to meet my dad."

CHAPTER EIGHTEEN

LYNNE

"You have no reason to believe me, Lynne. I swear I had no idea you were mine. I betrayed Richard's friendship. I barely remember that night with your mother. I woke up alone in my bed, but I knew something happened between Ellen and me. I couldn't remember much until I went downstairs and there she was, sitting at the table with your father and sisters having breakfast. Same thing, different day. She acted as if nothing happened when I knew it did. Her eyes gave it all away. She was secretively telling me we slept together and for me to keep my mouth shut. That bitch sat there pretending to be his doting wife while guilt hit me from every direction." Resentment sidles up my neck for a woman who has kept me from knowing my dad. It charges an electric current under my ass for her. God, how can she have all this control over people and get away with it? It makes me want to ram my fist down her throat and pull out her manipulative black heart. *I'm coming for you, mother!*

Matthew and I have been sitting on a bench a short ways down the beach for over an hour now. I've told him the ugly truth. All of it. From losing Tyson, to why I distanced myself from my family, to adopting. I even tried to lighten things up by teasing him for not being able to come to my wedding due to a high-profile case he was working on.

When Tyson first told me, I was stunned silent. The impact of Tyson's words stole every wisp of air out of my lungs. I don't feel that anymore. I'm breathing and sitting next to the man who helped bring me into this world. A good, kind man who I have always adored. A man whose hair color I inherited. Kindness and compassion for others. Among other things that will reveal themselves in time. I'm sure of it.

"She should have had the decency to talk to you about it. I hope you didn't feel guilty for long." I link our hands together. I want him to know that since I'm his daughter, he can feel me, too. He has to be angry, hurt, conflicted. I'm immune to the power my family holds. Matthew isn't. Not something as wrong as this. To withhold a man from his child. A child from her parent. It's the worst kind of wrong a person can do.

It also makes me realize that she without a doubt is aware of Jacob and Joshua. She has to know they exist. How could she not? I mean, it's a scandal, the same as this in her eyes. Another secret that must be hidden away. Good heavens. I'm beginning to wonder if she and Richard aren't in cohorts to see how many lives they can ruin just for the hell of it. A business proposition instead of marriage. Which I know isn't really a marriage at all. There has to be more. One missing piece to why either one of them would agree to keep secrets for the other, and as soon as we can find out what that is, we can put a quiet end to all of this.

"It took me quite some time to get past it. Your mother, she was flawless. Not at all the woman you've described her on our walk down here to be. Before that night, I used to tell Richard he was the dumbest fucker I knew to cheat on her. He didn't care. Always came back with the same thing. "You don't really know her. She's a bitch." Those were his words every single time.

"She was. Still is," I disclose sternly.

"She was never that way around me. Or around you girls. Every time I came out there, she treated me the same as before. This blows my mind. It pisses me off. I'm typically an honest man. Except for that one night. I don't regret it anymore. Not when the result of that night is you. I have never mentioned what happened between us to anyone. Your man, his friends. They are damn good at what they do. I couldn't believe it when I returned Tyson's call and he told me about this. They love you hard, Lynne. For them to dig this deep and find out about me and her from a wild hunch, then poke around LA until they found out she told your uncle about us. I couldn't be happier that you have a guy who would bury himself for you."

His admission of how my mother handled this hurts. My uncle as well. We've never been close to him. At least I haven't. When we were growing up, he lived in London. He moved back to LA several years ago when his health started to decline. The last I heard, my parents were forking out the money for him to live in assisted living. None of this newfound information hurts nearly as much as the painful impressions my mother has left on my heart. Those words aren't what stills me, makes me light up inside. It's what he's saying about Tyson. About me. He likes him. And this makes me incredibly happy.

"I'm glad you're here. Thank you for admitting that you care. You don't know how much it means to hear you say that."

"I've always cared about you, Lynne. Now, it's in a whole new light. I don't think I'll ever understand why your mother did this. Hell, she doted on all three of you girls when I was around. That lying bitch bent over backward for Richard even. That night, it's still foggy to me. But I need you to know, sweetheart, that the thought of you being mine never crossed my mind. Richard loved all three of you. He would carry on about each one of you. If he knew about the affair between her and me, he never brought it up, at least not to me. She didn't either. So, with everything you've told me, the only thing that makes sense to me is somewhere around the time you became sick is when he found out you weren't his." He has no idea that Richard never loved me, not like he did my sisters. Maybe he suspected I wasn't his. I have no idea. I don't really care what that son of a bitch feels or thinks anymore. All I'm trying to do right now is sit here and listen, rack my brain between this and the adoption. What it could mean, what I should do, and what Richard is going to do once he knows I've learned their dirty little secret.

That thought alone cleanses my soul. I am not related to that bastard.

My life makes sense to me now. At least the parts that have affected me the most. I'm not Richard's child. That's why he destroyed me the way he did. It was his way of revenge for my mother's betrayal.

"Has he ever acted differently toward you?" I ask out of curiosity. He edges his gaze back at me with an overflowing abundance of sadness; there's compassion there, too, love and guilt. Emotions swirl in his eyes; they rest heavily on his handsome features. I've always loved Matthew. He treated us like gold. Played with us and brought us gifts. I cherished those erasers he would bring me. The Statue of Liberty means freedom, and I relished in that word even when I was little and didn't quite understand the meaning of it. He even taught me how to ride a bike when my father had to leave suddenly to meet with a client. Kissed my scraped-up knees. It drives a hole in my chest that with everything going on right now I can't put him first. I can't get to know him the way I want to. I need to get through the shock, and I need to stay focused on those kids. They are my top priority right now.

I grip my pencil tight. I know he said we would erase and start anew. It boggles my mind as to how.

I silently cry when I realize that Matthew flew out here as soon as he could. He's making me his number one priority. The way a parent should with their child.

"No, he didn't. Richard is a smart man, Lynne. He also spends most of his time with actors and actresses. He's good at acting, sweetheart. Trust me, he knows I'm your dad." There's something about the word 'dad' that melts my heart. We always called Richard 'father.' I hated it. It seemed formal, not normal. But then again, my life has been anything but normal. Since as far back as I can remember, things were clear to me I wasn't like him. How true it is.

"My family. They all had to give blood when I was sick. Just in case I needed it. The only thing that makes sense is, he didn't match. That has to be it. How he found out," I exclaim. It's a hard punch to my gut; it stings and brings hurtful memories to the surface. None of that matters anymore. Not when I know this has to be why. This story keeps unraveling every day. It has to end somewhere. My God.

"Jesus Christ. You didn't need it, did you? Every time I called to check on you, they told me you were doing better every day." Guilt consumes the tiny little bubble Matthew and I have been in. It's eating him up. I've been there.

"No, I didn't. Guilt is not a factor here. You are not allowed to feel bad that he found out that way, and you most definitely will not hold on to it by you not being there. I received your cards and gifts. I wasn't in the right frame of mind to contact people. I didn't want anything to do with anyone. I don't believe in cheating. I lived with it for years. But look at us, Matthew. We have each other now. One thing I've learned through all of this is the importance of family. My blood family deserted me when I needed them the most. Family isn't always about blood. These past few weeks I've realized that more than anything. I'm similar to you in a lot of ways. In the few hours since I found out you were my dad, I've noticed our similarities. One of them is, I don't beat around the bush, either. Not anymore. Not after losing Tyson the way I did. Not after tricking my own mind into thinking I could fall in love with another man. We have so much to catch up on, and there are things I want to share with you. Things I want to know about you, too. I'm torn apart over this, Matthew. I don't want you to take this the wrong way. But I can't put emphasis on me right now. I have two little boys who need me more than they did before. This blessing in my life, that you are my dad, has to be handled in the right way. I need to speak to my lawyer, talk this over with Tyson. However,"—I take a deep breath, a hint of a smile holding the meaning behind my words—"the first thing I'm going to do when I see my mother is thank her for giving me you. For once in my life, I'm going to be selfish. I want you by my side when I bring them down."

"I will always be on your side. Anything you want. I wish I could have been there when you were sick." I stare into my dad's eyes. If I wasn't sitting down, I would be dropping to my knees, rocking like a baby. Because of these words. These beautiful words coming from him mean more to me than he will ever begin to know. I can't seem to express them. There's no more room in my brain for it to kick itself in gear and function.

For years, I studied to guide people through the thick, murky waters of their troubles. To help them rein in their fears. To assist them and to listen. Right now, though, I couldn't help myself if I tried. I'm not feeling pain. It's joy. It's a tremendous amount of it. So much that my vision impairs as it tries to wrap the sight in front of me into a tight little box to bring out in my memories whenever it wants.

"I want those boys, Matthew. I think between you, Tyson, and everyone else, we should be able to figure something out. Some way to push the state. They're either stalling or Richard has got someone in his pocket over there. I don't know. Something isn't right. My lawyer has called them, pleaded with them to come talk to me, and nothing. Tyson has called. Jude has his caseworker seeing what he can find out. I need help, please," I press. My voice ending on a whisper. I meant it when I said I would play dirty and I will.

"I'll do what I can. I don't have the pull here I do in New York. But I know the law, and it is not on his side. He's broken too many when it comes to those kids. You said you want them. How badly do you want them? Bad enough to take a drive with me to pay them a visit?"

***

"Tyson, I need to get up and shower, then thank Jude. I thanked you last night. Now, let me up," I joke, giggling as I try to stand to only be jerked back down, flipped over onto my stomach with my ass hiked in the air. He's on me within a second. Front to my back. His stubble is grazing my neck and warmth is scattering across my flesh.

A ridiculous voice inside my head wonders if I will ever be able to thank these guys enough for finding out about Matthew. I'm still on a high I've never been on before. I have a parent. One who loves me unconditionally, and no one is going to swing in and take that away from me.

Tyson pretty much dragged me into the house after Matthew and I returned last night. He was worried, and I should have told him I would be fine. And I am. I am better than fine. I'm graciously ecstatic.

I have never seen two men who barely know each other fit so well with one another. They didn't waste any time setting up a plan. One they didn't shut me out of. They included me in everything.

Tyson wasn't all that hyped up about me going to confront my family without him. On the other hand, once Matthew convinced him he wouldn't leave my side, he relented. I'm not afraid of Richard doing anything to hurt me physically. He's too smart for that. It's his words, the things he can do to me emotionally that could hurt. People say words shouldn't hurt. They do. They bite, sting, and then they blister. They bruise. Some last merely a second, others days, a lifetime.

He's a manipulator, and I need to get to him first before he takes Joshua and Jacob away from me.

"Later, I need in this tight pussy, Lynne. I want you to fuck my face. Ride my cock and soak my aching fingers." Those torrid thoughts are gone as I arch my back when he pulls my hair, slides a hand around and tweaks my nipple. I have no idea what's gotten into him these past few days, but I love the way his filthy talk and rough fingers awaken every part of me inside.

He's been non-stop talking, touching every chance he can get since Matthew and I walked back from the beach. We both have, really. It's a miracle he's allowed me to get out of bed at all.

I sigh. Focusing solely on him and how he makes me feel. What he does to heighten my body and take me out of the comfort zone I've been in when it comes to sex and seduce me with one touch to follow him into the danger zone.

"Holy shit, Tyson," I pant, my eyes rolling around in my head, my fingers clutching into the sheets as he licks a trail down my spine, pushes my legs open farther, and buries his face between my quivering thighs.

"This pussy on my fingers and tongue at the same time is fucking heaven," he growls, inserts a finger, and doesn't let up. He shows no mercy as the scruff from his face scrapes across my inner thighs, which heightens my desire. Combine that with his finger pumping fiercely in and out of me and his tongue doing exactly what he said, I feel my release start to climb.

He draws his finger out, inserts it back with another. My hands clench, my gasps fall from my mouth one after another.

"You going to come for me so I can get my cock in here?" His question shoots right to my core. I hit the roof with my release. My screams echoing, my pants increasing, and yet he still doesn't let up. He's attacking me in a way he never has before. Licking and sucking. Biting and nibbling my body until I'm on the verge of coming again.

And then he's gone, sliding up the bed, grabbing my waist, and begins to rub his hard, heavy cock between the cheeks of my ass.

"I could fuck you for hours. Stare at your gorgeous face for the rest of my life and none of it be enough. I love you so Goddamn much it makes my chest burn. Ride me." Our eyes meet in the early morning light. Lips parted. Intense.

"You are everything to me, Tyson." Never looking away from his gaze, I line him up, slowly sink down, and feel the familiar tingle of being stretched wide, yearning coursing through my veins. My core spasms, my soul bursts into flames, and I do as he wishes. I ride him; I watch him as he watches us connect. His heated eyes blaze brightly.

"Fuck, Lynne." His hands clamp around my waist. Up and down. Slow and fast. I feel his thighs clench. I want to close my eyes and ride out my own orgasm. I can't. I have never seen him look at me the way he is now. My heart is vowing to memorize this look forever. It beats wildly in my chest, consuming my upper body until I can barely breathe.

Tyson's eyes are telling me he is glad we are here. Our past is wiped away, and our future is in our grasp, and all I need to do is hang on a little bit longer.

CHAPTER NINETEEN

TYSON

I can hear Lynne, Matthew, and Maggie in the background as I slip back inside the side door of her house. My feet stop, my eyes widen as I take in the sight before me. The three of them are sitting close with their heads down. If they looked up, they would catch sight of me standing here mesmerized by the scene I'm witnessing. I can't seem to move to care if they did. To walk out there and tell them what I found out.

Un-fucking-believable. My mind is still reeling from what Jude and Riddick just told me. I was trained to deal with this. It's what I do, and my mind is locked down as if I were dealing with an emergency instead of the best news I've heard since Lynne and I got back together.

If a stranger were to walk up and take a look at them, they would appear to be a family intrigued by something. Finding it fascinating and truly paying attention to what each other is saying. Especially if one of them is his daughter. Damn. I wish I had something besides my phone to give Lynne this memory. She's happy. At least for the time being.

Lynne is pulling photos out of a box, staring at them in the same way she used to when we were younger. In amazement. Whatever they are, they mean something to her by the way her eyes are lit up and her lips spread wider with each photo she pulls out.

"These ones here were taken at our rehearsal dinner. I wish you could have been there, Matthew. Maybe things would have turned out differently if you were." I pinch my brows in confusion. For one, how the hell would that have made a difference, and two, she has photos of us? From our rehearsal? What the fuck? At least they better be from ours.

My mouth wants to override the memories of that night in my mind and ask to see them. She was flawless. A little nerved up. Still, there are times when I close my eyes and the vision of how she looked at me standing there as graceful as could be tears me up. She wasn't vowing to commit her life to me; she was saying good-bye.

"I wish I could have been. I definitely would have noticed the pain in your eyes. I'm surprised Tyson didn't." I did. I simply couldn't see past my own happiness to notice she was falling apart.

"He noticed. Except he thought it was nerves. At least that's what I led him to believe. I haven't looked at these in a few years. They always hurt me, reminded me what I had done. There were times when I missed him so much that I had to see him. These few photos are all I had to keep him fresh in my mind. This one here is my favorite of him," she says, skirting around the last night we saw each other, the last time I kissed her, told her I loved her and believed my life was finally right. I know exactly what picture she's referring to. She told me she was going to frame it. It's a simple instant polaroid snapshot her grandmother took of me watching her walk down the aisle. Shit. I can't hold back the tears that form. I let them fall. Wiping them away with the back of my hand.

The overwhelming rawness in her voice coils around my heart. It infuriates me and pulls the cord of resentment for the people who are responsible for it being there tight. It suffocates me, chokes me out, and has so many emotions swirling around me that I should have seen it. Her spark, her light was gone from her eyes. Goddamn it.

I refuse to stand here and take the blame. Not when the sources behind it all are closer to our grasp than before. I have always wanted to kill them for being a part of this. Nothing drives me to want to make them pay more than denying her the vision I see now. She's with her dad and a woman who adores her as if she's her daughter. Matthew's arm is slung across the back of the lounger, while Maggie's hand is on Lynne's knee. This has to end before I lock her away somewhere and wipe them off the face of this earth.

"Oh, sweetie, this is beautiful." I die a thousand deaths again when Maggie holds up the engagement ring I gave Lynne. My heart slams forward; it burns my entire upper body. Fuck.

"It's my engagement ring." Throbbing. Aching. Pain. So much of it in her voice, in my soul, that I can't stand here anymore. I slowly start to back away once again when the agony coming out of her stops me in a heated chaos of sensations.

"If we do get married, I don't want another one. I want this one. It means more to me than anything I own. They made me take it off, you know. The doctors, I mean. Before my surgery. I was so afraid I wouldn't get it back that I made one of the nurses promise me she wouldn't give it to my mother. I begged her to hold on to it until I felt it was safe to wear it. It never fit again after that. The chemo, my nerves. The grief. All of it combined caused me to lose weight. I tucked it away with everything else that reminded me of all that I'd lost." Jesus Christ. I'm gutted.

"God, Lynne." Matthew's voice is choking up. Fuck, I can't wait to get my hands on Richard. There is no wrapping your head around the kind of people who would hurt their child in the way she's been hurt.

"It's a new day. A new life for me. It's okay." It might be a new day, a new life, it sure the hell isn't okay.

"I better get cleaned up. Thanks for this. For stopping over, for being here." I watch her stand. Back slowly away with my hands tugging at my hair. My throat clogged. My emotions are draining the hell out of me.

Between this and what I found out, I could use an entire bottle of whiskey right about now.

"Hey. I was beginning to wonder what happened to you." Lynne and Matthew stroll into the kitchen, where she places the box that's taunting me on the counter as if she didn't more or less relive a hard time in her life.

"Just tying up a few loose strings from work." I pull out a bottle of water. Twist off the cap and down half of it. Pretending that her revelations didn't burn my chest like a branding iron.

"Give me an hour to get ready?"

"Take your time." I set the water down on the counter, cup Lynne's face, and kiss that mouth.

"I'm going to call the station. I'll wait for you down here," I lie, release her, and wait for her to leave the room.

I open the box, snatch out what I need, and close it back up. I'm too raw to look at pictures that will take me back to a place I'm trying to forget.

"Not a word." I point in Matthew's direction when he casts a suspicious eye my way.

"I didn't see a thing," he chuckles, holding his hands up in surrender.

Striding toward the back deck as quickly as I can, I make my way out of the house, across the street, and knock on Maggie's door.

"Tyson. Is something wrong?" Maggie smiles weakly.

"Not unless you tell me you can't do anything with this." I reach into my pocket, pull out the small black box that holds Lynne's ring, and hand it to her.

Her weakened smile fades; in its place is one that spreads across her face, hits her eyes, and pools them with tears.

"No tears. I can't stand to see women cry. Drives me to do batshit crazy stuff like this," I tease.

"Whatever. Come in." She moves to the side to allow me past. Shuts the door and snatches the box out of my hands.

"Won't lie to you, Maggie, I overheard the three of you a bit ago. Also, Lynne showed me the bracelets. She loves them. I think when, not if, I give this back to her, that it would mean more to her if she knew you had a part in it."

"I would love to help you, Tyson, but she said she wanted this one."

"I know. I'm not asking you to replace it with anything else. Not quite sure what I'm asking. This is a fresh start for us. Maybe you can add something to it. Change the design. Hell, I don't know. Something to make it memorable for her. This ring cost me a hundred dollars. The diamond is so small you can barely see it. I know she doesn't give a shit about that. I do. I want her to have more. She deserves to wear this ring, Maggie. It would mean a lot to me if you could do something with it to represent how strong she is."

"Dear God. I have never heard anything so beautifully spoken in my life. I'll do whatever I can to see her happy. I have the perfect idea in mind." She reinforces what I already recognize out of her. Maggie loves Lynne as much as I do.

"I appreciate it."

"I know you do, Tyson. You're a good man. How those people don't see that is beyond me."

"Yeah, well, those people don't fucking matter. You, however, do."

***

"He did what?" I stand abruptly. Peer over Thomas' desk and lose my shit. I have had enough of this. No more tail tucked between my legs. I've jumped off the cliff of being sane right onto the one of insanity. Headfirst.

Jude has tried, I've tried, we all have, and somehow Richard is able to influence the state to get them to jump through hoops for him.

The cop in me can't wait to get my hands on Richard. To tear him a new asshole. Prime that slimy piece of shit before he goes behind bars for good. There's one problem. I have yet to tell Lynne what I know, and as soon as I get my chance, I'm going to show Richard what it feels like to be interrogated by me. The rat that's been chewing away at my flesh for years has finally hit bone. It's payback time, and my hands are clenched.

"Sit down, Tyson, please?" Lynne's shaky voice does nothing to calm the anger rolling through me. I'm entirely consumed with it. Richard has backed her into a corner, and this is the last time he will ever try and get away with it. I suppose now would be the best time to tell them all what I know.

"Not until he explains to us how in the fuck he could allow this to happen. This is hypocritical bullshit, and you know it, Thomas." He better give me the correct answer or I'm knocking him on his ass.

"I didn't allow it to happen, Tyson. For fuck's sake. Look, I get that you all are going out of your minds. I am, too. Do you honestly think I've been sitting on my ass doing nothing? I've tried, Tyson. I don't have pull with the state and regardless what you think, neither does he.

They are giving him the opportunity to meet those kids. Unfortunately, they don't give a shit who he is or who you are. Their concern is for those kids, whether you want to believe it or not." *Not good enough, Thomas*. I'm about to dangle the truth of who I am right in front of their face.

"Concern, my fucking ass. Let's concern them with this. Right now, Richard is sitting in a jail cell. I doubt he'll be meeting anyone. Except for his lawyer."

"What?" Both Lynne and Thomas yell at the same time. I ignore Thomas' plea of 'why didn't you tell me.' Matthew says nothing. I filled him in the second I walked back in the house from seeing Maggie. I turn around, kneel in front of Lynne, and take hold of her hands. Christ. Her hands are cold and shaking, her entire body rigid, face pale.

"Richard has been arrested for drug trafficking."

"Oh, my God. How? I don't understand. He was always at his office. Always in court. How could he have time to deal drugs?" Her soft, pleading expression causes me physical pain. A part of me hates being the one to break this to her, while the part that loathes Richard more than anything is already crushing down on his black heart for finally fucking up in order to make revenge a bonus in her getting the kids.

"I'm sure he was, baby. He's what we call a middleman. He works directly with the big guys, takes the dealers' money and exchanges it for drugs. It's complicated to explain. Do you remember when I asked you if you trusted me?" She nods. I can see her mind shutting down, the reluctance to want to think anymore. I'm sure this is a shock to her. Hell, it was to me. I knew he was a crooked motherfucker, but this, never would I have thought the famous Richard Chapman would be involved in drugs.

I'll get my revenge on him as soon as I make sure Lynne gets hers. She's the only person I care about right now.

"You need to put all of that trust in us. In everything we've been through together. All of what you went through alone. I can't tell you everything. It's an ongoing investigation and no matter how much I want to stray away from my job in order to ease your pain, to take away the betrayal, I can't. He has to pay, Lynne. The one thing I can tell you is, you won't ever have to see him again."

CHAPTER TWENTY

LYNNE

I ignore the shrieking, the crying, and the shakes that are trying to take over my body. I knew today's meeting wasn't going to be one where I came out on top. I've been at the bottom for as long as I can remember. I've clawed my way to where I am now, and this turn of events has placed me right where I want to be. Close to the top. Close to having everything I've wanted.

I'm sitting here with my brain whipping all about trying to understand how a man who had everything at his feet once upon a time would get involved in drugs. He had a wife who I assume loved him enough to marry him. Daughters who would have done anything to seek out a father who would have given up anything to achieve one ounce of love from that man. How can this be?

"I vaguely recall anything after you told me about Richard. How is Matthew?" My thoughts are running rampant trying to recall what was said. There were whispers, a hand massaging the back of my neck, a phone ringing, and people milling in and out of Thomas' office. Beyond that, my body must have taken to the numbness as if a hundred tiny pricks of a needle hit my flesh. My mother and the man I've always thought of as my father are frauds. They've woven a web of self-destruction and in one swift sweep, everything they own will be wiped out.

"Similar to you. He's hurting more than he lets on. Losing his best friend the way he did has to be a giant blow. Bottom line, though, he loves you, Lynne. That one word is more powerful than any other. You should detect its meaning better than anyone." I release a slow exhale. I despise mixing love and hurt together. It's so cliché. And yet, it's true. Love hurts in all kinds of ways. It can heal, too. Makes people feel whole, fills them with goodness. Springs up on us all a craving since the day we are born. It's more than expensive clothes or designer shoes. Love is my new family and friends.

"Well, I don't associate that word with them. Not in the way Matthew did. This is a sick joke. The man must be devastated. Especially with him being a cop. God, Richard was probably selling it right under his nose." I'm trying hard not to hyperventilate in this truck. My chest aches for Matthew and how this must make him feel. Regardless of the love he has for me, it has to be eating away at his gut.

I hope Richard rots in his cell.

"Did he go back to the hotel?" I ask while unzipping my wristlet to bring out my phone to call him. My stomach bottoms out with worry for my dad. I pause mid-swipe when I realize what I called him. *My dad.* He's a wonderful man. We will get through this. Together.

"No. He went to the station to see about a job."

"A job. Here?" My jaw drops.

"Yeah. Don't act so surprised. What did you think he would do when this is all over? Go back to New York and forget he's lost thirty-one years with his daughter? I don't think so." I sink back into my seat. Today's events should have me shaken up, filled with rage and anger. Crusted over in darkness. Instead, I find myself feeling loved, cherished, and fortunate beyond the wealth I was raised in.

Richard never told me he loved me. He watched his money grow, gushed over Laney's artwork or Larissa's ability to learn foreign languages as quickly as she learned English. All he gave me was lies.

"I hadn't thought that far ahead. Life's been a little complex lately. For a while there I thought we were all going to go crazy." These past few weeks have populated us all with ambitions and doubt. Insecurities and craziness. It will continue on a few more days, weeks even, for Tyson and me until we have the kids and demolish my mother.

My dreams will not be short-lived this time. The jumbled-up pieces of my life are locked back together, while a sense of calm has wrapped around me. It's melted into my soul. Filling me. Consuming me.

Images of me as a young woman wounded from a broken heart flicker in front of my eyes. Hurt and humiliation are no longer present. It's all been suddenly replaced by anger toward my mother. A bubbling, boiling mass of blackness that takes me to a place I've never been before. Revenge. In the highest form.

Richard is going to be mutilated while sitting there spitting his blood all over the floor, and in doing so, I'll restrain myself from going to see him. Instead, I'll spend my time enjoying the boys while waiting for the adoption to go through. I'll sit back and let Tyson and the FBI clog up every artery in Richard's body. Make him gag on every lie, every treacherous, disloyal action he has performed.

Vengeance has come knocking, and it's not on my door.

"What are you thinking about over there?" Tyson asks smugly. He knows damn well what I'm thinking about. He just wants me to say it. I see the evil glaring out of his eyes. Hell, he's dripping with it. He's been waiting as long as I have to place a padlock over the only thing that will justifiably cause damage to the people he detests the most. Revenge. Except, I would assume he wants that lock to be dripping with the black blood that bleeds out of their dead souls.

"About Richard. I'm not shocked; I'm elated. Overjoyed that I won't have to look in his eyes again. To see his smug face when he tells me he took someone away from me. I'm still trying to figure out how I never saw any of it. You're sure my mother didn't have a clue?" My voice hardens with every word I punch out.

"I think she may have suspected. That's why she never left him. He may have threatened her. I can't be sure. Not until I talk to the FBI. One thing I am sure of is every asset they own is tied up. She'll be left with nothing. Not a dime to her name. I'll be honest. I was ready to say fuck all of the going by the book back at Thomas' office. My fingers were itching like a madman to call Riddick and Jude, to tell them to find an abandoned warehouse and tie him up until I got there. I want to kill him, Lynne, or fuck him up for life. A part of me wishes I could. Death is too good for him. He'll die in prison. I'll see to it."

I lean my head back, close my eyes, and laughter bursts forth inside of me. My mother. The Queen of the City of Angels is going to end up being the Queen of the Fallen. I can't wait to rub it in her face. To stampede her with the same phrases, stinging, hurtful words she used to say to me.

Her husband may be going away to live behind bars. But her, wherever she ends up will be the worst kind of hell. Scrambling her wicked brain to try and save her soul from falling. She'll never make it.

"How long will it take to get this information to the state?" I smile, knowing his answer by the way he smirks and narrows his eyes.

"Lynne. I may have waited until we were at Thomas' office to tell you. I sure as hell didn't wait to get that information where it needed to go. Jude and Riddick were taking it to them personally." My smile grows wider as a sense of self-importance washes over me. They've done all of this for me. For the boys. For Tyson.

"It seems I owe them another thank you." I tumble into a cloud of a dispute between my head and heart again. It's a foreign feeling to have friends. Especially ones who want your happiness and turn it into a mission to make it happen. To follow through with life's greatest pleasures without you knowing it.

"You don't owe anyone a thing."

"That's not entirely true. I owe Jacob and Joshua a life full of love. Of contentment. Stability. I'm going to teach them how to be better men. God, my stomach rolls with the mere thought of Richard raising them," I say disdainfully. I can feel the bile in my throat thinking what they may have turned into if he were able to. They could have turned out like him. Drugs could have corrupted them. Addiction. Prison or even death. I shiver from it.

Tyson lifts my hand, entwines our fingers, and presses a delicate kiss across my knuckles, and for one fleeting moment, my infuriation fades away as I look down softly smiling at how perfect my small hand fits into his. "I believe it's my job to turn them into men. Your determination to turn them into men turns me on. Though, I suspect we both better tone it down a bit, because there are a couple of kids along with their foster mother waiting to see who's sitting in this truck."

"What?" I reel my head around, and sure enough, my boys are standing on the porch with their mouths hanging open.

"Oh, well, in that case, I better step back and let you at them." I avert my gaze to where Tyson is adjusting himself; a soft giggle escapes my mouth. I've been so obsessed with my thoughts about the crumbling of a self-righteous empire that my mind slipped away from the most important people in this equation.

"Wait. Are we supposed to be here?" I frown.

"I don't give a shit if we are or not. I'm meeting those kids. Hop on out. I know you want to touch them." I do. I want to touch him, too. Tell him how blessed I am for having all three of them.

"I think they've grown." I yelp then spin back around and unhook my seatbelt. Even though I hear the deep chuckling coming from Tyson, I pay him nor it any attention. How can I when the minute I push open the door and climb out, I see two sets of eyes grow wider, hear loud screeching and words I'm not able to comprehend. I drop to my knees and embrace them both, inhaling that sweet, sweet innocence that surrounds them. They come so willingly, so eagerly. How could anyone not see that this bond we have was meant to be? A blind man could feel it; a deaf man could sense it. I'm not an idiot. I know unbridled love when I see it, and this is so far beyond it that it's insane. I kiss them, hug them, and hold them. I never want to let them go.

"I've missed you," I speak over the anxious babble droning out of their mouths. I wouldn't understand what they were saying to me even if it I didn't have more than I can handle rummaging through my head. My heart is literally blessed over this.

These children are everything. How can any man or woman hurt them? How can a person's conscious allow them to sleep at night? It's not about revenge for myself, for Tyson, or anyone else; it's them. They need me to protect them from a man who should show them nothing but love from the moment they were born.

It doesn't matter how many times I tell myself or the repetitious thoughts that scatter through my head on a daily basis. I will never understand it. Why people take the gift of love for granted. And I wish with all that is within me that I knew why. Love and family are everything. Life isn't complete without either one of them.

"Lynne, you're squishing me."

"Yeah, Lynne. I can't breathe."

"Oh, sorry. It's just, well, it's been a while since I've seen you. Can't a girl hug her two favorite boys?" I shrug, pull back, and admire them standing before me.

"Mr. Hill said we wouldn't be boys if we come and live with you. He said we have to be the men of the house."

"Jacob." His name falls from my mouth like a dishonest prayer. I regret more than anything having Theo and Jude explain that I'm working on them living with me. I should never have caved in to giving them false hope that they would eventually be living with me. It was my decision, but yet once again it was my family backing me into a corner. My shoulders sag, tears form in my eyes, and I'm suddenly at a loss for words. *Please, God. Let this work out. And hurry.*

"Well, I don't know about that. What if I want to be the man of the house?" Although my shoulders remain slumped forward and my heart is breaking for being no better than the people who raised me with their lies and dishonesty, I can't help but lift my head in order to witness them go utterly still. Their eyes are turning into giant saucers, and the only parts of their bodies moving are the shifting of two tiny little heads tilting up.

"Holy crap. Tyson. You are way bigger than you look on a computer. You're really huge. Did you bring your badge? Your gun? You said you would. Can we see it?" I would have dropped to my knees by the ambush to my tattered heart if I wasn't already. Joy compresses at my core. Relief sweeps me off the cool, crisp grass. I stand, place a hand on top of the boys' heads, and with a shaky breath, a tight sob wanting to erupt from within me, I observe Tyson drop down to eye level with Jacob and Joshua, open both of his hands, and display two shiny badges. That sob dislodges. I quickly stifle it by placing my hand over my mouth. I have never seen a more tear-jerking, heart-filled moment in my life.

Tyson thought I turned him on. He hasn't seen anything yet. There is nothing sexier than a man squatting down to give his undivided attention to children. He's enraptured with them, and I want him so badly I ache.

"You have two?" Joshua asks. I can't see their faces from here. It pains me. Part of the pain sketched on my soul erases within half of a pounding heartbeat. Just like Matthew promised it would when the gift I'm being given from the satisfaction spreads wide across Tyson's face.

"Nope. These are special badges. They need to be taken care of by someone who will watch over them for me. You guys wouldn't happen to know anyone who would want to keep them for a little while, would you?" At this moment, everything insubstantial dissipates. Even the air is trying to escape from my lungs. It is swooshing around in my chest, slowly. My pounding heart is the only thing permitting me to know that I'm breathing. Because everything else inside of me is numb. It's all washing away a lifetime of horrifying memories while relishing in one entirely spent up in my dreams. He's a natural at this. I told him he would be.

"We can hold them for you, can't we, little brother." My hand is still covering my mouth. A cry rips freely throughout my body. Jacob is always reminding Joshua that he's older. It's a good thing they are captivated with Tyson, because I'm more of a mess than the situation we are all in.

I take a step back. Circle my arms around me to stop the flutters from seeing a memorable sight forming in my stomach. I've had my share of quality time. It will never be enough. This time right here isn't for me. It's for them. For Tyson.

"I'm glad you stopped by. They've missed you." I refuse to take my eyes away from the three of them. The boys are holding the badges in their tiny little hands. Tyson is talking quietly, explaining to them what a special police badge means. I don't know what they mean or where he got them, but whatever it is has them nodding their heads in understanding.

"We should have called first. I'm sorry." I turn to face her. Her eyes are cautiously watching me. She's as nervous for them as I am.

"Your attorney called. I'm not going to ask you how you're holding up. I'm a little in the dark with everything that's going on. I'm not saying this for you to tell me your story, Lynne. As far as I'm concerned, they are yours already. I want you to know that we've told the social worker who came to see us that you love those kids more than anything and they should be with you." I want to scream right now. To throw a raging, childish fit. To fill her in on everything. To agree with her. I can't, and I never would. Not in front them. This dear, loving woman who opens her home to children who are left with nothing.

"My story doesn't matter anymore. They do."

CHAPTER TWENTY-ONE

TYSON

I'm sitting here nursing a beer while going over everything with Dominic. Explaining how strong Lynne was today. How every word she expressed punctured an entire set of holes through my heart. How they all beat against my skull until something inside of me snapped, causing me to want to drive straight to LA and put a bullet through that bastard's head. He tried to hurt her, and in the end, look where the arrogant man is now. Sitting in a jail cell just waiting for me to bury him underground.

My love for her and those boys kept me from going there today instead of tomorrow. All I can picture now is the way Jacob and Joshua lit up when I stepped out of the truck, badges in hand and concentrating on them. The way they talked, looked, and appeared to be strong when everything about them gave way to how much they love and miss her. How much they already care about me and how they've become an important part of my life.

There isn't a thing in this world I won't do to protect them. To give them the kind of life Lynne wants them to have.

I'm a man of my word. I live by honor, not pain. What kind of man would I be if I allowed them to be hurt? To be spotlighted because the same person who once hurt me wants nothing more than to hurt them, too. To pay a woman back for merely existing. In my mind's eye, I wouldn't be a man at all. I would be a selfish coward. And to the kids who someday I have faith I will be able to call my own, I wouldn't be the role model they deserve me to be. That's why they will never know who their biological father is. Not until we are ready to tell them.

"You're a good man, Tyson. Don't beat yourself up over not catching wind he was dealing, man. Hell, I had been watching him for weeks and not once did I see him step out of line."

"I'm beating myself up over him. He isn't worth it. I'm thankful the FBI got that punk taking and that Dietrich is kind enough to turn the other cheek for a few minutes tomorrow." I stop talking and glance over my shoulder to find Dane stomping in our direction, a tight scowl on his face.

I eye him warily as he takes a seat next to me. The fire in front of us is giving way to the stress, dark circles, and bruising around his eyes. Something is going on with him, and whatever that something is has nothing to do with the pictures he gave me.

"You doing alright, man? You look like shit." Dominic leans forward in his chair to face his brother. Dude is usually laid-back. Doesn't speak much, and yet now he's as worried if not more so than I am.

"I'm good. Tired, is all. Been running myself ragged lately." Damn liar. Either this drug dealing, cheating shit with Richard has really gotten to him, or there's something else going on. If I had to guess, it's something else. He hasn't had to do much. No one really has. Not like we all did when Cora and Vivian had hell on their backs. If anyone should be tired, it's Dominic. He's the one who's been running ragged following Richard everywhere.

Hearing this makes me feel like shit after what Dane told me a few weeks back about their sister. So, if there's a way I can pay both of these guys back for helping me out, then I know a good place to start.

"Tell you what. I have a place in the Coachella Valley. Not too many people know it's mine. That's where I went to clear my head a few months back. You can do some fishing, get wasted, and chill the fuck out. Your employees can run the business. They run into any problems, they can give me a call." Dane stares his brother down, runs his fingers across his chin in that I'm-thinking kind of way as he contemplates his answer.

"Works for me. How about you?" Dane shrugs like it's no big deal and turns to me instead.

"You toss in a couple good punches for us. Understand?" He lifts a brow, takes a swig of his beer, and quickly turns away from me. If I didn't know him well, I would think he was really pissed off at me. I love the guy, but I'm not going to push him to open up and tell me what's eating away at him. Maybe going away with his brother is what he needs. Get the hell out of here and work his shit out on his own.

"I'll be sure to send the message. Thanks for the help. You too, Dominic." I stand, dig in my pocket for the key to the house, twist it off the ring, toss it to Dominic, and rattle off the address.

We all turn at the sound of laughter. I'll never get tired of hearing it. Feeling it or seeing it. Maggie and Lynne are making their way toward us.

"We always have your back, man." Dominic's comeback is words every friend wants to hear. I give him a nod. Eyes are gesturing I'll have his if the time arises. Especially if he needs help with whatever is going down with his brother.

"You're a lucky fucker, you know that, right? Just from the few times I've talked to her, I can tell how much she loves you. Not sure if I've ever run across a love like that." Dane is sincere, but there's sorrow in his tone. He's feeding me another line of bullshit. He has run across a love like this. His own. Sucks like hell to see a grown man down. Never would have thought the way misery pours out of him like a rotten gutter was once me.

It's only been a month or so, but I'm a better man, stronger, weaker, more powerful than I can recall being. It's all for the love of a woman.

"I do know. You two have a good time." I shake their hands, watch them walk away, and admire the beautiful woman who stops to talk to them.

Lynne is all about simplicity and making things easy for the people she cares about. She could run her family's name through the dark, murky mud if she wanted. Unlike me, she'll use it as her last resort tomorrow when she visits her mother and sisters. Who knows what will happen. She'll poke the bear, make them beg before she finally wears them down and leaves them behind.

Lynne may have been fooled by them once, but she won't allow it to happen again. That could feasibly be why there's more of an easiness about her right now. The way she leans in and hugs both of the guys, her smile on those damn lips of hers that weaken me at the knees every time my eyes have the pleasure of looking at them. I'll take my last breath believing that the eyes are the window to a person's soul. But the mouth, especially hers, is the clearness that allows you to look through that window. For the mouth speaks what the eyes cannot. It tells your story, it speaks the truth. It expresses the lies you feel the need to voice in order to protect the ones you love. It provides everything that no other part of a person can, and I cannot wait to one day soon hear two simple words come out of hers.

"Hey, you two. Did you have a good time?" I grab Lynne by the waist, tug her to me for a kiss on that sexy little mouth. My dick jerks. Yeah, he wants that mouth. The two of them are becoming very familiar with one another.

"Yes. She finally broke down and showed me her secret. It's definitely not as easy as she says."

"It is if you don't stand there with the torch in your hand pretending that you're lighting it under your mother's ass instead of soldering the silver."

"She might need it tomorrow. Did you bring it?" I chuckle. The visual of Lynne doing just that in my mind. However, I'm hoping Maggie understands I'm not asking about the torch.

"Yes. I placed it under your pillow, you know, just in case you wanted to set fire to her ass."

"I'll set fire to her ass, alright. Come here." I grab the belt loop of her worn-out jeans, pulling her all the way to me.

"I'll talk to you tomorrow. Don't forget to slap the bitch for me."

***

A reflexive groan slips out of me when Lynne steps out of the bathroom, her ass swaying, her back long and sleek, and those toned legs have my dick getting all hysterical underneath the crisp, clean sheets.

"Jesus H. Christ. You trying to kill me?" I prop up against the headboard, adjusting myself for the second time today. "You better get your ass in this bed. He isn't going down this time." I toss the sheet off me, grab my length, and start stroking him up and down.

"Take your hand off that." She spins around and hell, my own slice of heaven. Her tits are perfect. Nipples erect and pert. Pussy right there in my line of sight.

"Get over here and make me," I taunt, slide my body down a smidge, and keep on stroking. I want in her pussy, but right now I want her mouth.

Her eyes divert down to my cock the same time mine shift to admire her mouth. I watch her, taking in the way her tongue darts out to lick her lips. I may love her pussy, her tits, her ass, but that mouth holds all the power. Its exotic beauty is endless. She can heal my soul with it. Steal my breath and make passionate promises of a sweet life to come. Right now, though, I want her to wrap it around my dick.

"Hand off," she repeats as she crawls up the bed to where I now have my legs parted to welcome her body to fit right where she needs to be. Warm lips attached to the greatest gift I've ever received glide up my shaft. My hand falls lax, my eyes roll to the back of my head.

Her weight shifts, her hands press into my thighs, and she takes my entire length in her mouth. Her head starts to move up and down. Damn.

"Sweet God," I groan out when she sucks my head, shifts her body once more, and I sink inside of her root to tip.

"I love you," she whispers, those words falling freely from her sweet, sweet mouth.

CHAPTER TWENTY-TWO

LYNNE

I've woken up more days in my life than I care to count with a dreaded worry that something terrible is going to happen. Although, as many times as my therapist tried to drill it out of my head, it remained there. Front and center and always ready to stab until my entire body clogged up with fear. Dread never failed me. Not through my cancer, my marriage, or the never-ending memories of Tyson that always hit me full force the minute I opened my eyes.

Today is a new day. Dread is no longer a diagnosis ranking my fear as my number one priority. Its persistence is gone. Replaced with a force much more powerful. Anticipation. I've worried myself sick over this discovery about drugs. The what ifs. Whatnots. And all that's in between. I've completely stopped worrying over something out of my control and buried in my past. Tyson and I vowed to take our steps forward, and after today, there will be no more looking back.

I've dreamt as many times as I've fantasized about having the strength to do what I'm about to do. To be able to take on my biggest fear, my largest dread, and put an end to its very existence. I just didn't know it was going to go down this way.

Tyson has done all of this for me. Making sure nothing is done outside of the book. The one he lives by. The one he took an oath for. He stood by his word, and I know with everything he stands for he will turn Jacob and Joshua into men they will be proud of. A man like him.

There's no doubt in my mind it's driving Tyson batshit crazy that I'm sitting in here without him when he knows better than anyone the fear I have. The dread I've lived with for years of being alone. Of having walls close in on me the way this tiny room has to be closing in on my mother.

Every part of me knows where he's heading right now. He's off to see Richard. To leave a permanent mark on his black soul. To show him that he isn't above the law. Tyson is the law. The good kind, the serving-the-people-of-your-country kind, and no matter how much revenge you want on a person or how much hatred you withhold in your heart for them, he's going to make Richard pay in the one way that's guaranteed to destroy him. A life behind bars.

People may think they are above the law, that they can walk around obliterating lives. Hurting, tainting, and poisoning their minds. They aren't. No one is. Eventually, it all catches up. Well, today I have a law of my own. And there isn't anyone in this small, confined room who's going to stop me.

I've done my civic duty by giving a statement regarding Richard to Agent Dietrich, and now as I sit at the long table and gaze into my mother's pale eyes, I want to laugh hard. So much so that it consumes me. It rips right through me and forces its way out in a childlike giggle.

"I believe I have a say in who comes to visit me. I demand you get them out of here, and in their place, I want my lawyer. What the hell is taking them so long?" she pronounces in her commanding tone to the female agent guarding the door. The same one she always used on me. I turn around and smile at the petite woman who says nothing. She crosses her arms, gives my mother a warning look, and stands her ground. *You have no authority here, mother. Oh, and your lawyers, my shit for brains brothers-in-law, are detained.* I'm not about to tell her they are being questioned a lot longer than I was. As they should be.

"And I believe you lost your rights to demand anything thirty-one years ago when my child was born. So, the way I see it, you have no say in a Goddamn thing. Not until you're arraigned. Even then you'll keep your mouth shut about us being here. And do you know why?" My dad stands, aligns his body, and leans over the table, giving me enough room to see her flinch. "Your life is about to change, Ellen. It isn't going to be pretty. Where you're going makes hell look like fun.

"Fuck you, Matthew."

"We did once, remember? I came here to thank you for it. For giving me the best gift a man could ask for. You are the dumbest bitch to walk this planet. You have no clue what you're up against, do you? Life behind bars is going to suck for you. You are going to be alone. Far more alone than my daughter was when you left her to fend for herself. You are going to piss and shit in a tiny little steel tank. Take a shower once a day if you're lucky. Eat food that others will spit in and sleep with one eye open out of fear." I blink back tears of joy. Laugh once again and lift my brows in a cunning way.

"I said fuck you, Matthew. You don't scare me. I'll get out of here, because I know nothing. Richard is a liar. He threatened me for years to keep my mouth shut. And you, you used me that night as much as I used you. How dare you come in here and accuse me of not telling you. What would you have done, huh? Whisked us away? Taken us back to New York to live on a cop's salary? God, you are as delusional as she is."

"That's enough." I stand, push out of my chair, and ball my fist. My swing comes out of all the pain, the anger, the tears, and the lies. It lands on the side of her head, and I watch her chair topple over, her head landing on the floor with a solid whack.

"You little bitch," she sneers from her position on the floor. Her hair a wild mess. Face void of makeup and eyes as deranged as she is. "You find this amusing, don't you, Lynne? The lost little girl who will never have a child of her own. The one who ran away when life became hard. Tell me, darling daughter, the one who fucked up my life, is this how you planned to see this all play out? To see me lying on the floor? Wanting me to grovel, to beg for your forgiveness? If it is, you may as well turn around and crawl back to your piece-of-shit boyfriend who put me here. Back to whatever road will lead you to nowhere in life, because I'm not telling you a thing. I'm not giving you closure. You will wonder why I've done the things I did for the rest of your pathetic life." The chains on her arms rattle as she shifts in her chair, eyes bugging out of her ugly, poisonous head. She looks tired. Worn out and pathetically ragged.

179

"I can handle her, Dad," I say when I notice him shift toward the end of the table. "She's nothing to me anymore. An empty womb, the same as me. The funny thing is, I may not have been blessed to have children of my own. What I do have is love, a life, and a man who loves me. A man who would never cheat on me. A man who will raise two children who aren't his simply because he wants to. I'm not here for closure. Closure would mean I love you, mother. Which I don't. I pity you and the lifestyle you've led. It's lonely and full of bullshit. I've never wanted anything from you but love. However, how can a person give it when it's clear they don't love themselves? What I'm here for is revenge. To sit here and watch you swallow every wrongdoing you have committed in your life. How does it feel, Ellen, to be surrounded by fear? You're scared, I know you are. You're also a liar, a thief, and you've stolen from me for the last time. Hell will never freeze over, so take my advice before you burn. Surely, you of all people need it when you're broken. When you don't have anything left in you to think for yourself. Tell them the truth. Tell them everything you know, and while you sit there in your cell, think about this pathetic daughter of yours. Me. The one who will be free of all the chains you've kept around me my entire life. You have nothing left. No money. No friends. No spa days. Not a single soul to help you. Take a look around this room and get used to it. There is nothing in here but gray walls and a black floor. Those are going to become your favorite colors. They suit you well." I pause and catch my breath. Clarity like I've never known before sits on my shoulders and rests there. Comfortably. And even though looking down at the clothes I have on isn't irrelevant, I find it quite amusing. My jeans are tattered and torn at the knee. My flip-flops obviously belonged to someone who loved bling; they were comfy and ninety-nine cents at Chelsea's Second-hand Closet. And my favorite piece of clothing is Tyson's Army t-shirt. It's big and hangs off my shoulder. If ever I looked like the woman I was meant to be, it's now.

"You have lost your mind. I should have had them lock you away instead of hoping that you would learn your lesson. That you would see that you can't make it on your own. You've always been weak, Lynne. Always. What makes you think you'll make it on your own?"

She's goading me. Wants to see me cry. Well, not this time. This time, I have four reasons to make it on my own. Four people who will stand by and watch me. I'm finally home. My life is bright and cheery. Soon to be full of two children's laughter, and those children will be mine.

"Jesus Christ, you're the one who needs to be locked away in a padded room. What the fuck is wrong with you?" my dad says from beside me.

"Shut up, Matthew. This is between my daughter and me. Richard used you the same way he used everyone else. The blind bastard that you are."

I become enraged. Book or no book, this woman needs to feel me for the rest of her miserable life. I sink down to the dirty floor. Turn my attention to the agent who smirks, turns her head, and looks away. God, I hate this woman. Her face is carved out of stone, the believability in her own philosophy on life dances wildly throughout her icy, storm-filled eyes.

"You listen to me, you crazy bitch." I grab her by the face and squeeze as hard as I can. "If you cared for anyone besides yourself, you would have taken your children and run. Threats or not. You would have found a way. Richard may have used all of us, but he used you, too. And you let him. You chose him over me, and now, because of your selfishness, you are left alone to pay." I release her and spit in her face. Stand with the assistance of a man who is far from blind.

"You don't know what you're talking about. You think that those boys won't turn out to be just like him? They have his blood running through their veins. They were corrupted upon conception. Are you really that desperate? I'm here to warn you that your children will turn on you the first chance they get. You did. You turned on us, for a man. What makes you think they won't do the same?"

"They may have his blood, but I don't. Tyson doesn't. He'll put them first. I will put them first. My friends will put them first. I will love them beyond anything, and I will never betray them, lie to them, or leave them when they need me the most. That's how I'll know. Have a nice life, mother."

"Lynne. I need your help. You can't leave me in here. I'm your mother. What about your sisters? You can't walk away from them. I need to see them. Call them, please." *Beg, Ellen.* It's such a lovely thing to hear.

"You were never my mother. They were never my sisters. You are all dead to me starting now."

When the door closes behind me, I tell myself it's the small moments, the soft touches, and a man who has me forgetting all of my pain and suffering from my past, because they love me for who I am. Not for what I can give them.

CHAPTER TWENTY-THREE

TYSON

I look over at Lynne. She's still asleep. Peacefully. The turmoil, excitement, and aggravation from yesterday's events weigh on my mind. I haven't slept at all. I'm not concerned about what's going to go down a few hours from now. Lynne can handle herself. She has it locked down. Her head is in the right place. It's with those kids and the unconditional love she has for them that makes her a powerful force to deal with.

I have no choice than to allow the first part of today to happen without being in that room with her. It's the only way. It's the right way. The way I'll be able to walk out of the Wilshire Federal Building proud to be a cop. Even though every nerve in my body is strung so tight it's impossible not to see me bleed, it's the best way to get our revenge. To bunker down and retaliate to assure her family stays out of her life forever. I'm a better man for it, and I thank every gorgeous hair on her head that she understood when I told her last night.

I reach over and touch her hair, my fingers gliding down the silky strands. She stirs. Her eyes start fluttering. I smirk. Can't help it. I wore her out last night. My cock is ready to go again. There isn't any feeling better than sinking inside of the woman you love. To move with her. To pleasure her in a way no one else can. It's a craving that never goes away. An itch that never fades.

Her eyes flick open, and it's right there in the early morning light that reflects all the love she has for me that shows me I'm doing the right thing by her.

I have to protect her, the boys, and my badge.

***

"Ten minutes, Corelli." I turn from the closed door behind which Lynne and Matthew are now with her mother and look into the sneaky, devilish eyes of Agent Rhodes, who I've worked with as many times as I've worked with Dietrich. The two of them are partners in this massive world of organized crime we all deal with on the daily.

As a narcotics officer, I've always enjoyed stepping through this very same door. To say good-bye to the assholes of the world. To completely turn the case over to the FBI before returning to the streets. In a sense, today is no different. Except, after all Lynne and I have been through, it is. I can't touch the son of a bitch like I want to. I can't beat his head into the ground. Cut out his tongue and shove it down his throat so he can eat every hurtful word he has said to Lynne. To me and everyone else. I can't even pull strings to give Matthew his chance at revenge. Not with Richard anyway.

However, I can make sure I haunt him. Install in the center of his skull the words that will drag him to hell and leave him burning with nowhere to go.

"Let's get this done," I emphasize, returning with an all-knowing gaze of my own. The need to rush back to Lynne as quickly as I can overrides the desire I have to slice this motherfucker up as I turn the knob and step inside. He may have taken away years from us, but after my ten minutes, he won't be stealing any more.

"What the hell is he doing here, and where are my lawyers? They should have been here by now. You're making this easier for me to walk with each passing second, you dumbass." I shrug, cross my arms over my chest, and hold his heated gaze. Every muscle in my arms is screaming to wipe that smirk off his face.

"No lawyer. Well, shit, this makes my case all the fucking better for me and a hell of a lot worse for you. You're royally fucked. I did see your protégés being escorted into a room. They'll be here shortly.

Which gives us plenty of time to talk." I'm going insane standing here. A crazed animal who finally has his target cornered. Fuck. I can smell him pissing himself from here.

"Remind me to cooperate with you guys more often, Agent. I'd appreciate if you'd give me a few minutes alone. This is personal." I've got years' worth of shit rolling around in my head, too much of it to care whether they forgot to mention he hasn't seen a lawyer yet or if he walked through that door right now. My guess is, there isn't anyone willing to touch him, not with the news of his cunt of a wife being arrested for the same charges he has. I swear to God I nearly tripped over myself when Dietrich showed me the file on the two of them.

They have more charges against them than any lawyer in their right mind is willing to take on. I'll bet my balls that's one of the reasons why he doesn't have one yet. The other being, he doesn't have a pot to piss in. No money to pay. And in this city, money talks.

"Your intimidation won't work on me, you piece of scum," Richard fiercely states.

"Not here to intimidate you, asshole. I'm here to send you to prison with a bang."

"You lay one finger on me, and you put a nail in your own coffin. Even a loser like you isn't that stupid. Or maybe you are. Being that you fell for a bastard child. We both know that's why you're here. To try and make me feel sorry for her, for you. Let me guess, it's going to go something like this. 'You never showed her any love, you pissed all over her childhood. What did she ever do to you?' She was fucking born, that's what she did to me. Let me make this visit easy on you, you fucking asshole. Do you honest to God think I didn't know she wasn't mine? Hell, I knew the minute that cunt of a wife brought her home from the hospital she wasn't." He stops talking, and my head is ready to explode. My stomach twists from the hate spewing out of his mouth. But he's not done. I can see the venom leaking from his brain and shooting straight to his mouth.

"For eighteen long years, I waited for the opportunity to crush that bitch. I prayed to the devil to give me something, anything, to knock her off her holier-than-thou pedestal. The scared little girl who thought she was too good for us. And then *you* came along. Turned her into a bigger bitch. Christ, I had to beg her mother to give Lynne the wedding she wanted so I could get her out of my house, being that the devil was taking his sweet time to answer. Then she got sick and every part of me wanted her to die. I could have let her. Believe me, I wanted to. Her mother went behind my back and sent her away, and for the most part, she stayed gone. Then all of a sudden, she came back for you and for those fucking kids." Hot-blooded fury floods my vision in the same way it did when I stared into the eyes of the enemy at war, knowing that if I didn't kill them first, they would slice my throat and move on to the next.

My entire body pulsates with unleashed rage.

"You are one sick fuck. Just like you, I've prayed for the day to come when I could watch you burn in hell. To sit back and observe you swallow your own shit. I could break your neck right now, but it won't be enough of a payback for me. Do you know what my vengeance is? The biggest settling of the scores? It's for me to live freely, motherfucker. For me to raise two boys with Lynne without her having to worry about you or her mother showing up and pretending to care. Lynne never loved you, either, asshole. Her hate for the both of you goes bone deep. The love she has for me, for those kids, and for Matthew is what makes her far from the woman you think she is." He tilts his head back and laughs. Cold, dark eyes return to fuel my feet forward. I lunge. Zero fucks are given about a book, because I'm going to fuck him up in a way that every time he moves, he's going to know what pain feels like. He's going to pray to his devil that whoever his lawyer ends up being finds a way for him to live in solitary confinement.

My fingers wrap around his throat and squeeze.

"Come on, you pussy. Do it. Hit me. Bruise me and make this easier for me. I know the law, and you're violating every one of my rights just by being here. When I get out of here, I'll get my boys. I'll sell them and laugh my ass off when she finally breaks."

"You don't have a clue who you're dealing with, do you? What was that you said about intimidation? You listen up, Richard. This isn't a threat, you son on a bitch. This is a promise. Your rights to those boys were terminated the day they were born. Your rights to anything have been stolen from you. Ripped from under your Goddamn feet. You fucked up, man. Fucked up big by giving Lori Lewis those drugs she took to kill herself. You voluntarily killed her. You knew she couldn't take whatever you had hanging over her anymore. See, I may be a loser. A lowlife piece of scum, but I know the law, too. Better than you do." I catch sight of his brain reminiscing before he does.

"You are so full of shit. That bitch was doing drugs the day I met her. It took me drying her out in rehab just so she could have those kids. I didn't force her to take them. She begged for them. Got down on her hands and knees and sucked my cock like she did every time she called me for more. She killed herself." And there it is. More recollection. More knowledge that he really does know the law. He just buried himself by confirming my wild guess. And it hits him full force the second I loosen my grip. I won.

"Did you get all that, Rhodes?" I ask while still keeping my hand around his neck he just hung himself by.

"You dirty, rotten motherfucker. You won't get away with this. There is not a chance in hell that will hold up." I release my grip. My job here is done.

"You alright?" I place my hands gently on the sides of Lynne's flushed face. She appears to be calm, much calmer than I am. I could have killed that bastard. Strung him up until all the blood rushed out of his cold, callous eyes and his disloyal mouth. Looking at her now, the warm expression in her eyes and the love that she has me shining like every sunrise we're going to spend together, I'm glad I went by the oath I took years ago instead of settling this score in the way that wouldn't have made me any better of a man than Richard is.

"Yes. I've never been better in my life. Let's go home. I'm assuming my home is your home now." She quirks a brow over those bright green eyes and that tempting mouth.

"Damn right it is."

EPILOGUE

One year later

"Come on, Grandpa, you promised." I look over to my father-in-law, who looks like the biggest idiot in the world with his bright yellow surfboard tucked under his arm, his stark white legs, and his Teenage Mutant Ninja Turtle's sunglasses on. I don't appear to look much better with my Batman glasses on, but at least my board isn't bright enough to blind me.

Surfing was never my thing. Not until my kids moved in. Now, I live in the water. Waiting on the swells of the waves, hoping for the big one to come. Feeling the rush as it swarms over my head and damn near drowns me. I can't get a grip on this surfing thing to save my ass, but my kids, they sure as hell know how to ride with their eyes wide open as the wave magnifies in size and their heads soaring into the clouds with all their dreams ahead of them.

It didn't take long for the state of California to sign away all parental rights from Richard. He didn't have a choice in the matter. As a matter of fact, he didn't have a say. He's rotting away for the rest of his life. Guilty on all charges, including negligent homicide.

So is her mother. The evil bitch. She'll die in that place from getting her hands dirty before her sentence is up. I'll guarantee it.

Both Lynne and I stayed away from the cases as much as we could.

Both of us had to testify. I'm used to it. She is not. The district attorney was able to convince the judge that when Richard and Ellen, who were both tried separately and without the help of their sons-in-law, came about, their lawyers would cross-examine her without bringing up anything related to the kids. It was irrelevant anyway. They were after Richard and her mother, not her. They wanted her credibility. Which, in hindsight, she knew nothing about the drugs, nor did she know anything about how the boys' biological mother got a hold of them to kill herself. However, what little bit of her testimony the judge allowed to their credibility as human beings left more than a shadow of doubt in the eyes of the jury.

Once both of the trials were over, her sisters tried with all they had to gain back the sister they lost. Lynne was done with them all. They lost the right to call her family the day she found out she was sick. We haven't heard from them in over three months now. I would have never allowed them anywhere near my family even if my wife wanted them. Well, that's not true. I would have, but I would have hated every second of it. Lynne is able to talk to her niece once a week. It's done behind her parents' back. I say what the fuck ever. If you're going to give your young kid a phone, then that's your problem if they sneak and call their aunt.

"You're not going out?" Matthew dips his eyes over his glasses to peer down at me.

"Not this time. They want you. I'll snag some pictures. God knows if I don't, Lynne will kick my ass when she gets home from work."

My wife has pictures everywhere. I have my favorites; she has hers. Although, every new picture we take becomes her new favorite. Mine will remain the same until the day I die. It sits on the nightstand next to our bed.

As long as I live, I will never forget the look on Lynne's face when the same day the boys came to live with us I got down on my knee right here in almost the same spot she walked up to me when I first found out she moved here. Maggie was with us, her dad, and the boys. I planned it all out. Finalized everything right down to having her face the house, where Vivian and Cora stood with cameras in their hands. Riddick,

Jude, Dane, and Dominic beside them.

When I opened the box and she saw the ring, she looked from me to Maggie. She knew. Maggie had spun her magic touch on my hundred-dollar ring and turned it into the most beautiful piece of jewelry I had seen. Maggie entwined the infinity symbol with tiny green stones that match Lynne's eyes all around the tiny diamond. Lynne fell to her knees in the sand and cried. So did I. I didn't care that tears were falling down my face; all I cared about was her saying yes. And when she did, I cried some more. I think we all did until the boys asked why we were crying. Then we all busted out laughing, and Lynne, the sweet, caring woman she is, took those boys in her embrace and explained the difference between happy tears and sad ones. Fuck, I love my wife.

Two weeks after that day was when she became Mrs. Tyson Corelli.

THE END.

Watch for Dane coming summer of 2017

OTHER BOOKS BY KATHY COOPMANS

The Shelter Me Series
Shelter Me
Rescue Me
Keep Me

The Contrite Duet
Contrite
Reprisal

The Syndicate Series
The Wrath of Cain
The Redemption of Roan
The Absolution of Aidan
The Deliverance of Dilan
Empire

The Elite Forces Series
Ice
Fire
Stone

The Saint Series
Riddick
Jude

Standalone
The Drifter

45488540R00112

Printed in Poland
by Amazon Fulfillment
Poland Sp. z o.o., Wrocław